REFUGEES OF CONFEDERATION

by

T.F. Pruden

Copyright © 2020 by T.F. Pruden

All rights reserved. No part of this manuscript may be reproduced, distributed, or transmitted in any form or by any means, including photocopying, recording, or other electronic or mechanical methods, without prior written permission of the author.

OTHER BOOKS BY T.F. PRUDEN

A Dog and His Boy

Grand Opening

One Fate Befalls

The Recalcitrant P.I.

Where Some Roads End

FIRST EDITION

Published 2022

by

Solitary Press

a division of

1986041 Alberta Ltd.

Cover

'Albert Street'

by

Lonigan Gilbert

T.F. PRUDEN

This is a work of fiction. Names, characters, places, or incidents either are products of the author's imagination or are used fictitiously. Any resemblance to actual events or locales or persons, living or dead, is entirely coincidental.

FOR MY GRANDCHILDREN AND THEIRS.

To Jake & Brenda Kaufman,

With warm regard from the author.

"Me–I will never give up." ~ Gabriel Dumont, 1837-1906

BLUFF

1

The first poker game I can recall took place around a green felt-covered folding table in my uncle Frank's basement. It was a few months after I turned seven years old. There, in fall sunlight cutting cigarette smoke into narrow grey strips through cheap plastic blinds, my father held cards with near a dozen relatives and friends.

As sure as I am sitting here today, despite the steady flow of often blue but always warm banter, a tension seeped from that table. To weave like an unseen thread through the house, trapping all it might find. Over the course of a lengthy afternoon, it wrapped those men and their families in a loose-knit blanket.

That varied in size, but was not ever pulled away.

From the shuffle of the first hand, I sat, quiet, on a low stool at my father's elbow. While there, I drank a queer mix of fear and suspense that seemed to spill, silent, from the table, unlike any I have since tasted. Meanwhile, the men around me guzzled beer and ate leftovers from a holiday meal served earlier by wives or girlfriends. While they won and lost amounts of money, even then I knew not one of them could afford.

The men at the table came and went as the afternoon passed. Those who lost either borrowed from winners at the table or cajoled extended family nearby for cash to get back into the friendly game.

For at least a few, there would be little, or perhaps nothing, left for tomorrow.

To the wide-open eyes of childhood, they all tried their best to seem unaware of that. It was like watching one of the old movies replaying on the console TV in the living room upstairs. Where my aunt Dorothy held the high ground, both moral and literal.

And there would have been many more children than adults spread about the rooms of the house that day. We mostly squabbled while forging lifetime bonds. Playing at something long since forgot with cousins in the home's unfinished basement, coming of the men first drew little notice.

I do not even remember who might have set up the folding table and chairs around which they were soon gathered.

So far as I know, though no one had yet called them the greatest generation, it seemed they should scarce disbelieve anyone who later did. At least, that is how it looks from here, a long way behind me with few left alive to challenge a child's fading memory. It may also be that I mistook bravado for confidence. But, even among brown folks as poor as we were then, a streak of near palpable optimism, that would be uncommon today, could be found. And for the life of me, I cannot imagine where it might have gone.

Anyway, I recall the riffle of shuffled cards turning my head from chums at my side to drama about to unfold at the far end of that basement. From where us kids were seated; I could see my father. He wore a grin that looked much like the half-tamed orange tomcat who lived in our barn as he waited for the game to start.

A moment later, I stood close enough behind him to almost see over his shoulder.

Near at once, I recall him turning far enough to favor me with that smile. Tilting his head and extending only his lips to point, he looked to a backless stool a few feet away. I grabbed it and, seating myself close to him, was soon ready to watch the events about to unfold atop the table. He said nothing but winked and nodded to me before turning his gaze to cards and the people holding them.

My father married his best friend's widow a few years after a workplace accident claimed the gallant life a foreign war could not. Talk of this unknown friend was seldom heard. But, when under the control of strong drink, loving stories of courage or valor were sometimes shared with former comrades-in-arms. Of the blended family made by their marriage, he said little to me. Aside from telling me that despite different last names we were, in fact, nothing less than brothers and sisters.

The info was first asked for after schoolmates pointed out the clashing last names between our assorted siblings. If memory serves, his reply to my query was direct, though less than clear.

"You are brothers and sisters," he said, "your last names don't make any difference."

Years would pass before I learned enough family history to explain it. And maybe this is no surprise, the news came not from a parent, but an elder sibling.

Only later would another notion dawn.

But even then, knowing my life was owed to a generation's cheer for surviving global warfare, I cannot say it cost me any joy found living it. This despite showing up at the tail end of an unheard boom, less a joyous reflex than an ill-timed afterthought.

Anyway, we were as unaware of coming failure as those before us were aware of their good fortune. And being selfish seemed a harmless childhood habit. Besides, I doubt anyone thought it would later prove a defining trait of either me or my cohort.

But I did not figure any of that out until long after it could do me any good.

And soon enough spellbound by an unspoken but clear struggle, I watched as the men played the game. I also tried to study my father, and though I could neither see his face nor make sense of them, I could look at his cards. He emitted a weird power as the pile of bills in front of him grew. While neither his speech nor demeanor changed, there next to him, it seemed I could feel his body temperature rise and fall with the stakes.

An hour swiftly passed, and on the faces of the men seated around him, even I noticed changes in response to the cards they were dealt. After watching for a while, to me it seemed my father placed bets because of their conduct, rather than on cards he might hold.

I cannot say for sure, but the habit might have been awaiting only a first drink to blossom inside me.

At the same time, though little seemed out of the usual to me, in the world beyond great changes of which I would know nothing hurried to remake a society in which, unaware, I then lived. Out there, in a world yet made of mystery, a summer of love waited on a horizon unseen, with but fragile distance to protect us from onrushing change.

Anyway, since watching it that day, I have pretty much been hooked on the game. Though it should also be said, it was little more than a hobby pursued among cousins or close friends, at rare times, until late in my teens. As by the time I came to know him, my father was a working man who had long ago departed the outlaw business. In those days, it was extended family and old friends behind most of the extra-legal action tied to our sprawling clan. And like it was for many poor brown folks of our time, much of the younger generation would soon move off the farm or the reserve. Before turning to the streets in search of a way out of the poverty trap.

So, only after moving into the city for work would I learn of the game's promise when played for serious money among strangers. In a short time, I then became known, in the places where it mattered, as a fellow who enjoyed a money game.

And gambling was illegal most everywhere outside a distant oasis in the American desert back then. But a rounder's word is all it took to get into private clubs running in the windswept prairie towns I called home.

An up-and-coming member of a clan well known for playing it, long before they made the game legal in most places, I was earning a piece of my living playing poker.

By the time I reached my thirties, the handle I used in those places had changed. Though if asked, few of the people at most joints where I was a regular player or even a club member would likely have known my name.

2

I did not know it then, but living the way my father liked was not much different from life in the eighteen-nineties. This despite the nineteen-sixties being more than half gone by the time I recall the first of my own memories.

To this day, the mental pictures of life out there are far sweeter than the brutal reality we endured before escaping it. Though of course, there are also folks who claim I have always been sentimental. And while they are entitled to the opinions, I did not get into this racket looking to argue with anyone about it.

Besides, there is no sense denying the effect of place and time on a person's life. So, I will not claim growing up like that did not play a big part in setting what became my life's course. But do not think I am looking to excuse anything I have done. At least, not because of some bullshit emotional or mental damage that later caused me to either misfit or malfunction.

Like most every young person living in Canada then, I received the benefit of a taxpayer-funded public-school education.

And much as it did not then, schooling Indigenous children either on or off reserve changes little of what they are taught today. For each gets the same whitewashed racism and bigotry told to all of Canada's white or immigrant students.

So, despite what I have since learned about the supposed free lunch, to claim ignorance forced me down the path that later composed my future would be a lie.

You should also beware, what I am hoping to tell you relies on a pile of notes made by a younger version of myself. Thus, it composes but one perspective on many unknown facts. And I will not hazard a guess about what anyone else living in that place during those times might think of them.

After spending most of a lifetime safeguarding the treasure, however, I am grateful to have thus relieved myself from the remorseless freedom of flimsy memory.

He was a man who enjoyed having things his own way. And living nearest the fringe of the civilized world was his choice. For he rejected many values of the place then encroaching upon his beloved backwoods.

Whose comforts already included such miracles as the telephone, electricity, television, and modern machinery.

One is not hard-pressed to guess at the many contrasts between our lives and that of even close neighbors. Without so much as a gravel road reaching the place until after I left it, he paid relatives or friends to foster us so we could go to school.

Upon starting classes at a farming town nearby, the difference between us and our fellows was not only plain, but subject to scorn. Surprised by their rejection, I recall telling of ill-manners and attempts at bullying by new school mates on a first weekend visit home.

Besides not fitting in, exposure to the world outside via the marvel of TV and a post-modern schoolhouse would soon give rise to many other questions.

I should also say that about most subjects, my father kept his replies as simple and direct as his grasp of language allowed. He was known as a fellow who much preferred a smile despite being resolute and ever willing to respond in kind.

We were not then expert foster children and not used to listening to family celebrate from the darkness of a distant bedroom. I cannot speak for siblings, but holidays and similar events would thereafter border on painful for me.

The complaints were made in a rush of fearful anger too long held back. After listening to his sons that day, with the younger of the two struggling to hold back tears and the older wearing a fat lip, he pronounced swift judgement.

He spoke calmly while looking directly at me.

"Next time someone tries f***ing with you or your brother," he said, "take a club and knock the sonofabitch down."

With that, he lifted my brother in one immense paw to carry him in the crook of an elbow and, grabbing my hand with the other, led us into the cabin. Which he built himself and we then called our home.

"Come on," he said, "let's eat. I don't know about you boys, but battling always made me hungry."

To this day, I have not forgotten that lesson. From time to time since, it has been necessary to survival. And I remain grateful most to the man who taught it.

3

All the same, I would leave the safety of my father's house to seek my fortune at the tender age of fifteen years. Even today, I cannot claim so much as the semblance of a plan to support the irrational act, beyond bold desire to have my own way.

As it had for the father, such deeds would prove hallmark of his son.

Because of our nearness to the Arctic Circle, in most years the growing season was barely long enough for cereal crops where we lived in western Canada. But summer days were lengthy, and my father's homestead bordered a reserve placed between two big lakes near the center of Manitoba.

On a map, the place is nearest to one edge of the rocky Canadian Shield. Known as the Interlake district, it is a land where muskeg breeds an endless torrent of bloodthirsty blackflies. While summer heat often climbs near triple digits. And the cool relief of an evening breeze coincides with a nightly plague of ravenous mosquitoes. In numbers enough to deny even the minor delight of exposing so much as an inch of bare skin.

That such a place could bring routine winter cold of forty degrees below zero for weeks on end, should be no surprise. And though believed a winter playground by weekend ice-fishers on the many lakes causing the bone-aching January humidity, life under such terms can seem baffling to a local.

To the North waits endless miles of bog-filled and near opaque Boreal Forest. Broken up by countless lakes. Followed by the open Tundra of Canada's once frozen Artic. Much of the so-called farmland in the region, however, amounts to low sand hills covered in scrub oak. And split by rock-infested strips of thin topsoil. The soil in many places barely covers near impenetrable clay. Divided by river and choked by low-lying swamp, most of the reserve's ground is barely suited for pasture. And, partly because of dams built to bring hydropower to a capital city far to the South, the reserve was also cursed by routine spring flooding.

Over decades, the annual spring floods devolved into a de facto make-work project embraced by locals.

In time, a regime in charge of government budgets assigned to the long-term problem of annual local rebuilds also grew. After a while, as wages and working conditions improved, concern for jobs would overtake that of stopping the annual floods.

As most often happens, the seeds of dependence were sown with best intention.

The case gives an effective model of paternal colonial powers at work. For they had moved the Indigenous people now living there, from southern homelands. Under terms of peace treaties signed with a foreign Crown.

It was a scene repeated throughout the place called British North America.

And in their place came settlers from eastern provinces and foreign lands to reap the long-term benefits. While, in exchange for empty promises of freedom and equity in the place that would become Canada, its first owners ceded control of the most valuable real estate within the new country's borders.

Aside from a few Metis rebels, who were easily enough quelled. With soldiers and a single hanging.

Most times, moving the people took place without a shot fired.

From either anger or celebration.

While old news to many, I repeat it here as a reminder history lives in the hearts and minds of the people. No matter how many windy revisions might be published by those holding power over them.

And like it still does for those who cannot afford it, a wet summer meant disaster for farmers small and large in the days before crop insurance. My family belonged to the former camp and the year I left home was unusual wet.

I spent two long months working for a ranching outfit managed by an uncle a hundred miles from home that summer. And well understood how bad things were likely to be for us because of what had been near endless rain across the prairies. There are few things worse than wet weather during haying season for a mixed farmer, aside from more of it come harvest time. For small farmers and their families, such a confluence of circumstance can easily lead to failure.

Through much of the working season that year, to stave off bankruptcy, my father also labored off the farm. Soon it was no longer necessary to wonder how bad things were, as most of our cattle were sold as the hay ran out. With neither feed nor money to purchase it at prices driven by scarcity, it was either that; or keep them to starve.

I returned home the Friday before Canada's labor-day long weekend. It was Sunday afternoon before my father stopped in on the way back to work. He drove a pickup truck owned by the neighbor then employing him and carried a whisky bottle when he entered the cabin. As he poured himself a drink while greeting me with too-easy praise, it was clear he was at least half in the bag.

Even before opening my mouth, I knew it was a piss-poor time for talking.

But after a summer on my own doing a man's work for top wages, I had a new feel for the world and my place in it. And by then, the idea of going back to a life spent under someone else's rule had been rankling me for weeks. With school also waiting only days away, the thought of listening to some bored teacher drone held less allure than finding a job in the city and making more of the money I had already learned to enjoy.

The mystery of a world beyond our lonely farm had, by then, made a home in my imagination. I will not deny it now.

Unknown to me, my father suffered while fighting to keep the legacy he hoped most to leave his ignorant sons. I would not figure that out until much later. Though if I had known, I am also not sure how much it might have changed.

Like it or not, a time had arrived, and just then there seemed no postponing it.

"When did you get back?"

He sat at the kitchen table with the opened bottle of whisky and a pair of dented steel thermos bottle tops in front of him. I did not have to look inside of them to know what they held. One was for plain water; the other he half-filled with amber liquid.

"A couple days ago," I said, "got a lift from Uncle George."

I tossed an envelope thick with half my summer wages in cash onto the table.

"How much are you contributing there?"

He did not touch the envelope.

"Half."

"You're a good son," he said.

I knew he must be quite drunk to talk like that, and a knot tied itself up where my stomach used to be.

"I'm leaving," I said.

He drank from both rough cups, before replying. Though not intending purposeful defiance, I stood only a few feet from the table, near looming over him.

"Leaving where?" he said, "What are you talking about now?"

He raised a single eyebrow, tilting his head slightly as he looked up at me.

"Leaving here," I said, "got a job waiting for me in the city."

That was a lie. Because, at the time, I did not understand even the basic seasonal nature of the tradesman's labor market.

"Bullshit."

He spoke in a voice that betrayed little but mild surprise. I think he might have scowled, but he neither moved nor raised it.

"You've got school starting next week."

"I've got a drywalling gig starts next Monday at Winnipeg," I said, "and we need the money, don't we?"

Now, before I go on, it may be worth saying that under the circumstances, most anyone might find his patience stretched. After all, loss of a life's work is not something anyone imagines. The boozing was a response to the pressure of being confronted by it and even then, I should have known that.

Or maybe being scolded by his teenage kid pushed him over some line. I know there is not one shred of blame held against him for what came next. He was the closest thing to a hero I would ever have and remains so to this day.

But, staying true to himself, my father responded in kind.

When I awoke moments later, he was gone. And, near as I could tell, a backhanded cuff had knocked me out. Though it first seemed I was not badly concussed. I bled from a cut to my lower lip. A glance into the mirror above the washstand showed a bruised cheek with a bit of swelling. It happened so fast I am not sure if I even flinched before it was over.

To this day, his uncanny speed and animal's power impress me.

After wiping my face and packing a grip, I walked out. Less than four miles of gravel later, I hitched a first ride.

We would neither see one another nor speak for five years.

4

I scribbled a first note to my boyhood self on the night of that poker game. Over the decades since I have written countless, not unlike it. Most often in point form, using the broken scrawl I still recognize as coming from my own hand. Stored haphazardly at best, they were collected, but remained unread as years passed. Whatever my intent, it seemed manifesting their unknown purpose would prove beyond my grasp. But habits are soon hard to break, and once begun it persisted despite either protest or circumstance.

Unbid, the writer's life welled from a source unseen within me, though I remained unaware of it for quite a long while.

The province's capital city waited more than a hundred miles south of my father's home. And while a bus served the remote northern communities, it also followed a posted schedule. My thumb got me there before midnight. To find a poker game underway at the home of a surprised eldest brother. Where multiple cousins and friends greeted me with offers of food, drinks, and sofas on which to sleep. Not only tired but unsure of myself, I begged off the game to instead crash overnight in a spare bedroom.

When I awoke next morning, the comfortable and furnished rental apartment in a renovated two-story Victorian four-plex was empty.

Sadly, I failed to keep the note my brother left for me on a spotless kitchen table. Not yet sixteen, within hours of arriving, a full-time job was mine. It was the first of countless breaks my eldest brother would give or create for me over the following decades. A working stiff like his father, he was yet a rounder struggling with addiction then. And despite the boundless courage of ignorant youth, now and then frightened me.

Most often when boozing, which I would soon find out he did on a regular basis.

And I do not need to look at notes to recall the joyous relief of those early days working at the big city day job. For wages three times what I had earned before it. A crew of cousins and friends laughed among themselves while doing their best to keep me from hurting myself. As I rushed to justify my place as low man on the totem pole.

"Relax my bud," he said, "we need you here, you don't have to impress anybody."

We stood next to one another at the open trunk of his battered sedan. Each of us covered in crusted sweat and drywall dust in the fading heat of a late September afternoon. He tossed a tool belt into the box waiting there and I followed suit. A moment later, he placed a calloused but affectionate hand on my rapidly broadening shoulder.

"You're his son and already as good as two men," he said, "you'll make the rest of us look bad if you don't slow down, ok?"

He smiled while speaking.

Shamed at being called a keener, I hung my head.

"Sorry," I said.

My voice emerged as a strangled croak.

Near at once, he squeezed my shoulder and laughed.

"Don't worry about it," he said, "you're making your old brother look good. Now come on, let's get some dinner. I want to hit a game for an hour or two tonight."

I did not go with him to the game that night. Nor would I follow him to any of the clubs for several months. From that moment, however, I watched his work habits closely. And modeled my actions to follow that of the men around me as we moved from one job site to another. Near at once, it was clear my brother and the other tradesmen adjusted their pace to match the changing demands of both task and time.

Over those next months, the life of a postmodern construction site revealed itself like an unfolding puzzle, as deadly and careless as it was marvelous and complex. Staying alive and safe in such a place is a challenge.

But, with help from my brother and the men working with him, the many worksites cost me little aside from a few aching muscles. While also paying well for a youngster without ties. And within hours of starting the job as a drywaller's helper, I understood why trade apprenticeships took four years to complete.

Even then, a skilled farmhand, capable horseman and equipment operator, the talents called for by the trades near derailed me at first. Already a well-trained young athlete, muscles, and tendons I did not know existed greeted me with shouts of misery each morning through those early weeks of hard labor.

To this day, I remain grateful to my eldest brother for the boyhood times spent as part of those crews of working men.

Because, like I said before, he had other demons. And though he would eventually near destroy himself before slaying them, it is not that story I am telling.

5

"So," he said, "I guess it's just you and me, young fellow."

The last man between me and my first big pot sat with head cocked to one side and hands folded together upon a flat stomach. A pair of hole cards lay face down on the table in front of him, along with enough money to take me out with a single bet. He was no stranger to me and well known at the private club where I had come to play my first game with professionals.

Dressed casually, with flawless style, he wore a relaxed grin and seemed every inch a pleasant enough character. Owner of an impressive physique, though less than average height, his wide shoulders and thick arms ended in powerful but calloused hands. Perhaps approaching middle thirties, the skin of his face bore few lines save those caused by the smile.

A large stack of bills now lay before him, for he ran roughshod over the game at once upon joining it. Despite their losses, not only the dealer but the other men at the table clearly enjoyed having him there.

This time, my cash lay at the center of the table. I remember thinking back to the years of lessons my eldest brother drilled into my head. And hoping no one else could feel the shaking of my belly as the hand unfolded.

"There's only one way to play this game," he said, "and don't forget it. No matter what, if you can't raise, you have to fold."

The sharply dressed man had played at least three quarters of the hands dealt since joining the game an hour earlier. During the same period, I played only my few blinds, in each case mucking unplayable cards at the first over bet. More than a gambler with his luck running hot, the fellow also impressed by turning over monsters when called by an assortment of solid players in earlier hands. As he sat behind me at the table, besides skill, the advantage of last move also belonged to him.

All the same, though he called each of my bets, it seemed near certain I must now hold the best cards.

In an instant, I reviewed the hand sequence in my mind, from arrival of my hole cards to exposure of an unsuited flop, Ace, Deuce, Three. Next had come the turn, bearing not but a certainly worthless Seven. And finally, the river card, where fell the second Deuce that should only improve my hand. For the life of me, I could not imagine why the fellow called as I raised the maximum with each round of betting.

In the hole sat the pair of bullets I had waited with exquisite patience to load before firing my first broadside at the pros seated around the table. As instructed, before and after the flop, I had also raised. With trips at the turn, only the stubborn fellow seated behind me hung around for the river card. Now, with two of us left and the big tight made, it seemed my choice was clear as crystal.

Despite a ten-twenty limit with three-raise maximum, the game was also table stakes, leaving the option for all-in bets on the river. Should the player wish it, a single bet could, in theory, end any hand, though rarely did.

With the best hand made at the turn, I could not imagine why the older fellow stubbornly refused to muck his cards. In earlier play, he showed no wont for life as a calling station, either raising or folding according to his strategy.

Why then had he taken to calling max bets?

As it turned out, I made a few notes about the game later that night. In them, it says he looked at me with something like pity as I waited to take his money. It also notes things during the hand I should instead have noticed.

"All in," I said.

I leaned forward in my seat. And pushed the stack of bills in front of me toward the pile loosely collected at the center of a felt covered oval with seating for ten plus a dealer. The club was housed in the basement of a north-end Winnipeg butcher shop. A pungent aroma of curing meat hung in the air despite clouds of cigarette smoke. There were two tables, one for ten-twenty-table-stakes and the other reserved for three-six-nine with a three-raise limit. On that night, only a single game was underway.

"I call," he said.

I flipped the Aces waiting on the table in front of me.

"Aces full," I said.

I can still remember the smile spreading across my face as that long-forgotten dealer made his pronouncement.

"That looks like our winner," he said, "show us your hand, please sir."

The dealer instructed my opponent. He replied with a nod.

A veritable chorus of 'nice hand' and 'way to go, kid' rose from the men seated around the table. It not only surprised but embarrassed me.

The older fellow grinned from across the table, saying nothing as he surveyed my cards. Before slowly shaking his head. A moment later, he spoke.

"A good hand well played young man," he said, "but sadly, I've got two pair."

I first snorted in reply.

"Thanks," I said, "but a full house beats two pair."

The dealer, after counting the money I had pushed into the pot next looked at the older man and spoke.

"That's another two-fifty you've got to cover," he said, "for the all-in bet."

My opponent next spoke on, plainly quite pleased.

"Most of the time it does," he said.

He looked at me while speaking.

Then he grinned. Before flipping the pair of hole cards to reveal his hand.

"But not this time."

The dealer stopped counting.

"Because four of a kind beats a full house," my eldest brother said, "and I've got two pairs of Deuces."

6

A few of the men around the table called it a bad beat, but I would learn the difference between that and poor play. Though it took a while. It also cost plenty. As that rash bet was but the first of countless pricey mistakes.

Each made while learning the trade secrets needed to survive the routine swings of the poker table.

Because, like most who do not play it as a profession, I was yet blind to the nuances of a simple card game. For while enjoyed as a hobby at holiday gatherings, early returns among fellow amateurs proved middling at best. Always a front runner, the losing not only pissed me off but sparked a lingering desire for revenge.

Which, so it seems, is most often needed to provoke personal growth here.

One of the great believers in forgiveness, it is also certain forgetting is more than unusual in these parts.

And though rarely playing together in those earliest days, my eldest brother would promote the schooling. While easing the cost of his growing habit with the price of my failure at home lessons. As I would later discover, no matter when purchased, the price of such knowledge ever remains near seasonal highs. Much as the teenage cousins invited to play along with us also learned, it is a price most reliably borne by the young.

Having been lucky to live long enough to grow older, I remain grateful for the chance to pay it.

There is also no denying it took me longer to figure things out than it should have. But in those days, we lived without the now widely available books on the subject. And the now pervasive internet was yet an army's pipe dream.

Thus, it often seemed the only way to figure a thing out was by devoting oneself to practical study. As a result, mountains of net income produced by long-forgotten day jobs held from teens through twenties were flushed down the drain of an autodidact education.

From the earliest days, to me, it seemed too high a price for fun.

The private poker clubs then spread across the western prairies, most of them long gone, are not only my alma mater but that of more than a few members of the extended family. In those dens of inequity, many of us first learned the rules of a well-trod road and respect not only for the game, but its players. And much like his father before him, my elder brother was known and respected in many of those places. Where, despite lacking his charm, as younger sibling I would be allowed entrance to the clubs and welcomed to play. Though, at first, extended no credit.

And I was also fortunate, as early visits took place before I could raise the entry fee.

So, from a seat at the rail, and for several weeks, I watched before sitting down at my first game with them. They played three-six-nine Hold Em. And unlike my oldest brother, it was soon enough clear I lacked the single talent needed to win among either skilled or professional poker players. For despite extensive schooling in most of the game's finer points, it was near at once plain that I suffered from an illness for which there was no cure.

Of course, there were also few options, such as legal or lawful outs, available to me should I have wished to instead pursue them. Because, though plainly white-passing, I remained brown enough on the inside to resent life as a little Eichmann.

So, while unhealthy habits seemed ready to keep me on a fast-lane chase for easy money and good times, at the outer edge of my often-wired awareness, few choices waited. And pursuit of anything beyond crime or construction would take the courage of a solo effort, plus both talent and time. Of those two, not even the latter seemed available to me. Despite knowing fast times seldom last, it was looking then like I should be content to see where they led.

Anyway, it turned out I was one of those poor souls able only to play cards, not the people holding them.

7

At this writing, Manitoba's capital city of Winnipeg has long been home to the province's largest local population. Once, it seemed overrun with three-story walk-ups filled with what was called 'old world' craftsmanship. Which included stuff like brick construction, lathe-and-plaster walls and ceilings, and miles of old growth hardwood. By the time I turned up there, rents were cheap and urban renewal had yet to replace all that tasteful elegance.

Along with much of the city's charm.

Many of those apartments were built either before or between wars fought earlier in the century elsewhere. Most featured solid wood trim with an authentic lacquer finish. That old-growth lumber was beautiful. And seemed only more so if joined by tongue-and-groove oak floors with a hand-coved ceiling in local work of that vintage. When split with a paring knife hurled by an angry young woman twenty feet away, however, the trim emits a crack much like a shot from a twenty-two-caliber rifle.

I report this using the voice of experience.

As I recall it now, though reaching a then current common-law wife's boiling point was not rare, use of the knife marked a certain upturn. In later years, a wiser fellow would accept such acts as final notice. Back then, it seemed little more than much enjoyed passion, soon assuaged with whispered nothings and slapping bellies.

Such is the glory of ignorant youth.

The grey-and-white cat, a rescue six months earlier and by then well-loved and quite spoiled, purred between us. We lay together on a king-sized waterbed in the bedroom of a high-rise apartment we shared. It was newer and lacked the charm of our first place. Located across the street from Winnipeg's tiny Central Park, the penthouse one-bedroom lacked a balcony. Just then, stoned on a couple of hits of Orange-Double-Barrel acid scored from a cousin, it seemed good fortune.

"Ever wonder what goes through that cat's mind?"

I lay on my side, near certain I could not move. Next to me, she raised an eyebrow, but paused before replying.

"You think Pusscat has a mind?"

She smiled, rubbing the cat's belly. Blue eyes, oceans deep but not so clear, and long white-blonde hair. Tanned, fit, and filled with youthful promise.

"I guess I've wondered."

She stopped stroking the cat for a moment, then reached out and touched my cheek. An acid-shudder passed through me as her fingers traced the side of my face.

"You need to relax, honey," she said, "Pusscat doesn't have a mind."

I grinned as the light in the room seemed to flicker from sunflower's yellow to a bloody red, then changed rapidly between a grassy green and the dawn's sky blue, before returning to what I hoped, of a sudden, must be the alabaster glow of normal.

"Are you sure?"

She tangled her fingers in my long hair. Like fireworks on Canada Day, a million sparks seemed at once to erupt from beneath my scalp.

"Don't worry," she said.

Her voice seemed to echo in the room.

"Pusscat is just Pusscat."

And I was not there when my father first spoke the definite

words about me. But over the years, he would often be granted cause to repeat them. And when he should, most times, the audience to whom he spoke could only nod in agreement.

Many times, I would also be forced to hear it direct from the horse's mouth.

"The boy is c**t crazy," he said, "and there's no cure for that."

Maybe he was not entirely mistaken.

What is sure is that I have always loved the ladies. And it seems they have been kind enough to return the favor a time or two. But there is no denying that from the start, my ways have tried the patience of many a long-suffering paramour.

Nowadays, friends in the know politely refer to me as a confirmed bachelor.

As it happened, I would shack up with a rebelling blonde from the Garden City neighborhood within eighteen months of hitting town, sure it was forever. I am also quite certain neither of us had yet voted when we met at a party thrown by someone lost to memory's shifting sand. What I do recall is, after ending up in her bed later that morning, I never got around to going back to my eldest brother's place.

Equally sure, after her first one-night stand, she would stake everything to the lost cause of my badly needed reform.

There is a chance I would not have forgotten either her beauty or those times, but notes prevent memory of sweet youth from dulling reality's jagged edge. And for each night of passion would later fall a flood of tears. So, and despite what has been claimed about loving, I doubt either of us much treasure the loss.

But, in those days, it seemed like everyone was doing it.

As I recall it now, poor folks once believed living together by rule of the common law a real option to legal marriage. Though I cannot speak to its vogue since community property laws were accepted and enforced by the courts.

For young men untouched by wealth such as myself back then, however, the sexual revolution was manna from heaven.

Made by modern birth control, it soon led to a buffet of sexual choices not before seen in polite society. A combo of fluid public morals and eased parental controls dished up what then seemed endless freedom to review new life partners.

In depth.

The generational cynicism resulting from it was but collateral damage.

After three days and nights away without so much as a phone call, she had good reason to be pissed when I walked in that night. Besides, if she had not been doing dishes, it is doubtful the knife would have been in her hand. Though a glance revealed the stubby blade buried and quivering near an inch deep in the door's trim. Anyway, it seemed more reflex than a planned attempt to cause me harm.

All the same, I ducked into the hallway bathroom before she had time to reload.

"Miserable sonofabitch!"

Her voice was more scream than shout.

"Where the f**k were you?"

I should also point out that she neither cursed nor seemed to know how when we met. Well, not long after shacking up with me, I had given her plenty of reasons to learn. And while the one-sided chat that next took place is long forgotten, one memory lingers.

A shrill tone, which for the life of me I had not heard before that moment, also seemed to just then enter her voice. And I will not deny that afterwards, the sound of it would not leave my head. In a display of the fickle facts of either young love or human nature, that unfriendly tone would sour what, until then, I recall as a most pleasing love affair. And no amount of either sweat-soaked sheets or shared sunrises could thereafter convince me staying with her was worth its price.

Not eighteen months after getting together, we split the blanket.

Though unaware of it, the breakup also ended my best effort at early reform.

8

The six months of jail time demanded by my first pinch were suspended in exchange for a medium sized fine. Plus, a list of conditions with which I retain limited recall. I was lucky to run into a judiciary going liberal along with the rest of us. Chief among the demands was avoiding crime and those committing it.

As extended family then made up most of my close friendships, many of them would prove unenforceable.

By then already well-schooled in the workings of the legal system, I knew the score about as well as the judge. Slapped on the wrist for covering up a school friend's drunken insurance fraud, punishment for the attempted commercial crime would only later impede my life's progress.

And so, the wheel turns.

My younger brother took no joy from the game of poker and would play little at home. Only if pestered was he convinced to join the usual holiday games. Which is good fortune, as the boy showed little talent aside from an ironclad nerve. That seemed to arrive as birthright along with the last name.

Despite unsure virtue, as with siblings, it would prove durable.

And much like the rest of us, he was greatly affected by our father's love for horses. But in his youngest child's case, it manifested in a taste for the racetrack and the legal gambling found there. For though a quiet fellow when compared to elders, the younger brother was subject to both weakness and demons of similar force.

He was also cursed by the gift of art. As natural as breath itself, it spilled from pencil or brush whenever he might take either in hand. Though to a fault sensitive, his place among the boisterous pack was that of treasured but vicious golden child. Secured by a temper of volcanic scale backed with rigorous athletic training.

Amid a bad bunch, the youngest brother made up for lack of physical size with indelible commitment and practiced skill. Early and committed disgust with the world and his place in it not only informed the art, but drove him to a decorated amateur boxing career. Which gave little aside from teaching him to apply brutality. Fortunately, he would thereafter vent either anger or energy into training for life in the squared circle.

Though semi-regular in following him to the gym, I would ever prefer ripping off a picket to breaking a hand when forced to defend myself. Furthermore, as not only the lover of tail but also a player of percentage, the gamble of combat is foreign to my nature.

For there are no sure things in either, that I learned early.

Only every once in a long while could he convince me to join him at the track. When it should happen, it would only cost me nothing but money. Which he considered the price of his company. Though he did not say so out loud. And in those days, I enjoyed it well enough to pay the cost.

The local racetrack opened a few years before I was born. On the western edge of the prairie city, a six-and-one-half furlong oval featured thoroughbred racing from May through September in those days. Along with grandstand seating for five thousand. And despite the legendary prairie cold, harness racing was then offered through the winter months.

As with most gigs, there are few things a gambler enjoys more than a chance to ply his trade. By then, whether aware of it or not, both my younger brother and I moved closer to earning the infamous status.

Through the months after that first pinch, fear of the cost of lawyers more than respect for colleagues kept me out of the poker clubs. Bored close enough to death as a result, I then spent more weekend afternoons than usual in the company of my younger brother. Watching as the horses ran. Looking back, it proved an expensive break from what I believed a hard-earned and much-preferred skill set.

To this day, handicapping the horseraces is beyond me.

And those years spent in the saddle are no help.

But, when I turned up there, my younger brother already knew people. And they seemed to know others with a finger on the pulse of the track. My notes reveal a stream of people making daily contact with him, few known to me.

Despite growing up in the same place and living in quite a small town, we moved in different circles.

But like I said, little aside from losses are recorded from those times, showing my lack of appreciation for the so-called sport of kings. Even now, I most recall that early split from the poker table as lonely. Deprived of a by then needed fix, the track proved little more than a pricey substitute.

And day jobs, despite the wanted pay cheques, were rapidly losing their allure.

9

Partly because of increased traffic with the local police, I left town before that suspended sentence was fully served. The track bored me. And there were few other hobbies practiced in those days. Aside from hanging around the boxing gym swapping knuckles with pros for five dollars a round. I was, at best, a bored sparring partner. So, even my younger brother supported the plan for a geographic cure.

If only to save me from taking more of the brain damage I could scarce afford.

From where I stood at the time, leaving town came with conditions. Once again shacked up with another one and only, dreams beyond my own should doubtless pay the price of an unplanned solo departure. The latest petite and blue-eyed blonde then sharing my bed had other ideas, and daddy issues paved the way for us to remain together.

"Well, good luck with that," he said, "I'm thinking you're going to need it."

I nodded before speaking. And hoped he would not later be proved correct.

"Thanks," I said, "and let's hope for plenty."

We stood next to each other in front of a crudely painted wood bench. In the steam filled locker room of the Winnipeg Boxing Club. Surrounded by men from bantam through heavyweight leaving or heading in for training. While toweling off, we continued a chat begun in the dank communal showers. With each of us then known well enough by most frequenting the airless gym housed beneath a cold storage company warehouse, our chat was regularly broken by 'heys' and 'howareyas' from passing fighters.

"You didn't forget she's a waitress?"

I met her when hired as a doorman at a local nightclub.

"Nope," I said, "she's a good worker."

He nodded while rubbing behind an ear with a semi-white cotton towel.

"Well," he said, "I guess it's handy for cash flow if nothing else."

I was busy for a moment, pulling on faded blue jeans and a loose tee shirt. While trying not to let anything touch the slick mildew covering what had once been white paint. That now flaked from a chipped concrete floor.

"I'm not planning to get broke," I said, "but she knows the score."

He made a frown while looking at me as he buttoned the crisp bowling shirt. Which he wore above faded jeans. A moment later, we sat next to each other on the bench to pull on near identical white socks and running shoes.

I recall several more intrusions.

But soon enough, we escaped the malodorous subterranean crucible for the cooling breeze of a high summer afternoon.

"So long as you don't forget what the old guy told us about waitresses," he said.

Stung by the comment, I could only chuckle at the memory.

A few months before, he stood next to me with beer in hand near the lady's room entrance in the club where I plied my trade as doorman. From a spot prized by those in the field, a complete review of the joint's female patrons was possible. Like most in those days, we made little attempt to disguise an ongoing critique.

The waitress in question drew lustful glances from each of us whenever she passed by with a tray in hand. Despite years spent at the poker table, there could be no hiding the intent behind what amounted to borderline sexual harassment. Nor that she played along with it, cheering me on though affairs between staff members were frowned on by the club.

After only two weeks on the job, it was clear to everyone working at the joint we should not long resist a shared want.

"She's hot stuff," he said, "but don't forget."

The voice was gruff.

A regular customer, older than both of us put together, staggered up. He placed a hand on my shoulder to steady himself. Though wearing an expensive three-piece suit and in good cheer, he seemed much the worse for wear. He weaved slightly as he stood there.

I smiled and placed a reassuring hand on his back before speaking.

"What's that, Kenny?"

I also leaned close to his ear while talking.

With a nod and a wink, he crooked a finger toward the younger brother standing next to me, to show he should come closer. With an eyebrow-raised glance my brother leaned in. To better listen to wisdom proffered by the well-dressed elder known to us both only by unplanned association. Now through waiting and with pregnant glee, more than loud enough to be heard above music blaring from a nearby dance floor, the grey-haired drunkard hailed forth his learned teaching.

"Look up waitress in a dictionary," he said, "it says, 'see Jezebel'!"

This time, he shouted.

The old sonofabitch then threw back his head to emit a foul cackle of guttural laughter to which my notes grant no justice. No lie, the remark took us by surprise and for a minute it seemed likely my younger brother might piss his pants.

Hell, it says here I near split mine laughing as well. And despite supposed enlightenment gained since, the old bastard's words put a smile on my face to this day.

Never one with much concern for appearances, it should also be said that many a budding romance was derailed by family of numerous partners over the years.

In most cases, my lack of attention to or outright ignorance of the basic social graces led to argument, if not outright disgust. Add the usual concerns about race and money to the ingredient list and a recipe for trouble near creates itself.

There is also no denying a strong prejudice for young ladies of Caucasian background survives in these parts.

Anyway, between the waitress and I, extended family waited to greet us no matter where we might travel. For at about the same time, the siren of Canada's only locale untouched by winter's annual misery called. Its grey skies and green grass waved to us like fool's gold at the western end of a national rainbow.

Though I did not know it, getting there would prove most of the fun.

And so long as I have one, memories of a too brief time together will haunt with dreams of what might have been. Of course, as they must also compete with recollections of what took place outside the bedroom, I am saved much pain.

For not three months after moving into a North Shore place together, during a couple's holiday weekend at Kelowna, hosted by her sister, a pattern would play out. Due perhaps to a dispute but most likely to my arrogance, within twenty-four hours the sibling could find little to admire in my gal's choice of mate.

A raised eyebrow and questions suited only to family left her with a lingering discomfort. No matter how that hardworking girl fought to deny it.

Not even early departure could stop the sprouting of a seed of discontent now resident in the hearts of once innocent lovers.

Here is what I mean. In the beginning, we spoke to each other all the beautiful fictions men and women share when they are in love. At the end, we told each other all the terrible facts the same two people know, when they no longer feel that way.

And soon enough, it was plain to her that living with me would ever come without guarantees, no matter the place. So, not six months after making our home among the over-ripe fruit of a semi-tropical urban wasteland, the heartbreak of common-law divorce once again showed up for breakfast.

10

Sure, I can laugh now, but maybe it is worth pointing out that young love most often sells for an unreasonable price.

Anyway, much like her brothers, my elder sister was a known and respected rounder. She had long roots in the business of sex and drugs. And she moved to Vancouver before I was old enough to vote. There, she ran her own show. While keeping herself clear of the gangs who owned the east side of western Canada's largest international seaport.

To her, I will ever owe more than can be told.

But there is also no doubt that she supported my reform, if only by showing the many perils of an outlaw lifestyle. As by the time I made it out there, legalized casino gambling had already spread across the western provinces.

Overnight, local buffets of chance guarded by wolves long starved of it opened their doors to a clueless public. For pros well-schooled in handling newbies, an early feeding frenzy should also have proved instructive.

Though as usual, placing bets on the future was an unknown math for most people. No matter what heartless formula was tried.

And not long after I got there, my sister arranged a gig for me tending bar. At a dive frequented by most of the dealers, Johns, junkies, trannies and working girls supporting the local sex trade on East Hastings. With concerns about everything to do with the ghetto gig but sky-high North Shore rent to pay, I recall having little room for complaint. As I soon found out, many frequenting the gay bar were either friends or associates of my sister. That later went out of their way to ease me into the perilous neighborhood.

Because working down there could seem like being trapped in a violent action movie playing out in real time. The joint, like the streets outside of it, was filled with plenty of cartoonish low lives. But many authentic gangsters, stinking of threats better read about in pulp fiction or laughed at on TV, also hung around the place. With most running one criminal game or another, danger traveled with them.

Even now, I recall being cautious when coming and going. And choosing my words with more than usual care in everyday chat. In less than eight weeks, however, my working stake was rebuilt by generous tips from people plying a bounty of dangerous trades. And to this day, I remain grateful for that.

All the same, I recollect not a single tear falling when I was at last able to walk out of that joint after a lengthy final shift.

But in times before the currently widespread internet, word of mouth stood as the usual choice of info-sourcing for the rounder on the street. Fresh players either moving in or passing through most cities found much of what they needed to know from similar places. The game of choice made little difference, be it gambling, drugs, sex, or any of the daylight world's many prohibitions.

For the limitless power of a network was known long before lonely nerds monetized digital porn and called it the world wide web.

And though I was unaware of it, my sister turned her first trick while still a child to feed her younger siblings. It was not long after our parent's marriage crumbled. A life thereafter called whenever times turned tough. And the old wives' tale of slipping down a slope is based in heartless fact. Thus, she had been forced to accept the job long before growing old enough to understand what it meant to choose.

It is not only this world's oldest gig but remains among the most dangerous.

And seemed always to be around while growing up among poor folks. Not in plain sight so much as rumored to be available. Selling sex, to me, seemed close enough to a licit profession back then. My sister was far from a solo example within the extended clan. She learned of it from elder relations also involved in the heartless trade. I am no longer sure when I first remember the oddly routine comings and goings.

But it was some time before writing notes became a habit.

Nor can I recall any member of the extended family talking or saying anything about our many relatives' criminal acts when gathered for occasions.

Later, teenage partying brought me into contact with my sister at work. I accepted her gig without question.

Underage when first surrounded by a buffet of sexual talent, my early carnal schooling would be gained because of relief granted by her colleagues. Born of ignorant want but nurtured by learned pleasure, I am pleased to report a lifelong respect for people working the thankless sex trade lives in these parts.

11

The cousin who introduced me to the owner of a local private social club also made his living by the sex trade. As it turned out, the club's operator had a taste for the occasional wild side escape from the routine delights of a lengthy marriage. Upon hearing I passed no judgement about such matters he was happy enough to extend a player's membership not long after meeting at the gay bar.

Though without the earned privilege of house credit.

My notes reveal great pleasure at the first step taken to establish needed local bona fides.

Already well-schooled in the danger of markers, it is near a sure thing I would not have taken one if offered. By then, it was usual for me to start small in a new place and I was playing only lower limit casino games topping out at five-ten with a three-bet limit in those days.

And to those in the know, action at a three-six-nine table with such a raise limit is the better payer. For like about everything else, poker is played according to levels best assigned by ascending skill than increasing stakes.

Due to its lower betting limit, the three-six-nine table attracts players of lesser skill. In those times as before, pros understood this and only in the worst of times took advantage of it.

The game though illegal and underground not only survived but grew because of this respect paid by those relying on it for their living.

As not much more than an apprentice, I then believed a three-six-nine game the best match for both skill and wallet. The first time playing at the private club, however, located a lengthy drive east along the King George Highway and into Surrey, would prove little more than a break-even affair. But, not for nothing is it noted from tiny acorns grow the mighty oak. And though I did not know it, that first private game out there would again change things for me. Because somehow, and I swear without my noticing it, the damned thing went on for a week.

I would later note the time spent sitting in that friendly but evil joint as my first real experience with a different kind of fever.

Housed in the basement of a strip mall with a hidden entry found only via the back lane, it was early on a Saturday morning when the locked steel security door buzzed to open. Not visible at the back of a covered parking garage unless you knew where to look, the owner told me to share my new member's card with a giant standing beside a counter.

Behind which a young woman with a weathered look waited to check coats. He was a mountain covered in tattoos while her dress left modesty in the closet.

A natural light-heavyweight known to walk around closer to one-ninety in those days, my large hand disappeared when he shook it.

"Put the kid's jacket in with mine, Jackie," he said.

The girl with the tired face smiled as she took my coat. She handed me a blue disk with a number stamped onto it in exchange for an expensive leather.

"Look out for this guy, Lil'," he said, "he's a tough player."

He spoke to the giant.

The giant nodded to him in reply. He then looked down to me with a deferent grin.

"Pleased to meet you," I said, "and thanks."

Another pair of smiles, accompanied by reassuring nods, plainly delivered by rote, was their joint reply.

I next followed my host down another three steps and through a set of sliding doors into a well-lit and air-conditioned space.

Where a half dozen of the standard ten-position-plus-dealer poker tables lined either side of a lengthy and well-finished basement. A pair of counter-height rails created a wide aisle down the center of the thickly carpeted room.

At the distant end, what amounted to a café operated. Two small tables sat on either side of a wide hole cut into the wall and outfitted with a melamine countertop. Above it loomed a plastic-lettered menu board.

While, at each of the tables, a game was underway.

"Higher limits and table stakes on the left," he said.

He gestured with the appropriate hand to indicate the tables on that side of the room.

"Lower bets and three raise limits on the right."

I nodded but made no reply, instead noting that despite a low ceiling and the steady hum of shuffling chips mixed with table-talk, the room seemed to emit little sound. A glance overhead revealed an acoustic tiled ceiling, also regularly vented. Without windows and bright lit by covered fluorescent tubes, soon after walking into the room a sense of being disconnected set in, as though it could be any hour of the day or night.

Just as, when walking up to the place after parking on the street out front, there had been no sign of it.

"Kitchen is open twenty-four hours," he said, "but Charlie don't cook anything that isn't on the menu."

Though grinning when he spoke the caution, a glimpse at the enormous and menacing cook standing behind the counter caused me to at once make note of it.

"Sheets on the flops are changed every morning," he said, "and there're free towels for the shower."

He pointed to a door right of the kitchen, then closed. Behind it, I later found a large room with six single beds and a night light. Plus, a bathroom with shower and plenty of hot water. I remember growing ever more impressed by the joint and its service as a mid-forty's waitress hustled past with a full tray. She was on the way to a high limit game at the far end of the room.

"Washrooms on the other side," he said.

This time he waved to show a pair of marked doors to the left of the café's counter.

"We're not affiliated," he said, "but it's members only, weapons are turned over at entry and either Little Willy, who you met, or his cousin Big Ray work the door and keep things calm in here."

I nodded my respect for the specimen at the entrance, wondering a moment at the size of a behemoth his family called Big Ray.

Above each table along the finished walls of the large room hung a bevy of cheap prints in expensive frames. With poker the shared subject, most showed dogs using several well-known cheating techniques. As we walked the length of the room together, the owner stopped at about every other game, introducing me to players I have long since forgotten.

At each table, however, the greeting was easily as sincere and warm to him as it was cool and appraising of me.

And near at once, the plainly dangerous place felt like home.

12

But that instant comfort did not come without its price. I did not call until late the first Sunday evening, near two days after getting to the place. Already sick of my habits, by the time I made it home a week later she had abandoned the North Vancouver studio for a bedroom at her mother's home in Surrey.

And despite a real and lingering heartbreak, the apartment remained my home only so long as it took to square away a joint closer to the lower mainland action.

Which, perhaps due to what then seemed a habit, proved too easy.

Anyway, times being what they usually are for gamblers and their ilk, it was not long before I was shacked up with a blackjack dealer working at one of the Burnaby casinos. With both tolerance for and trust in my nocturnal habits, the serious work of earning while learning flourished under the routine cover of what passed for domestic bliss. Another good earner, she also managed the expenses when losing streaks reduced me to case cash in those early days.

And though I can no longer recall her name, I remain grateful for the support.

But do not get the wrong idea, because despite the demands of my addiction I held a series of 'day jobs' either tending bar or dealing poker in those days. I also will not deny there were months when tips paid the bills due to sloppy and ineffectual gambling at 'house games' with tilted odds like roulette and blackjack.

So, we must have been together six months before I gave serious thought to playing full time, and that many more before I believed myself ready for it.

The near endless notes leftover makes clear an ongoing problem that would confront me throughout my career. For at no time would math knowledge, learned by rote despite not finishing school, prove able to overcome it. As a result, the well-earned rep of a tight player then dogging me came not by choice. To anyone with a lick of sense watching, it was necessary to survival.

Because it seemed no matter where the game, it was most often played by sharks with teeth far sharper than mine.

And though I would remain mostly ignorant of it, a boom was breaking out and coming change was in the wind. Not long after making it back from a losing trip to the American desert, a rough week among the local sharps convinced me to join my brother for his weekly game.

Told it was filled with wealthy amateurs, I recall my biggest fear being the legendary cold weather reputed to infest distant Edmonton.

Even by then, I should have known better.

13

The first time I got serious broke was during a snowstorm spent among the wild-west gamblers found there, at ice-bound Edmonton. As everyone who ever turned a card for cash knows, it is also a well-known hazard of the work.

So, if you play for a living and it has not happened yet, keep going and you are sure to find out.

The fellow hosting the game was as nice a player as any I would ever meet. In time, I would learn more than a few lessons from him. Though not long after sitting down around a second-floor boardroom table above his company storefront and offices at a Northside industrial park, his play had me rethinking the choice. Between him and my eldest brother, it was no game for a greenhorn. Only the presence of a half dozen well-heeled players of lesser skill kept me from cutting what appeared near certain future losses.

As by then, I had learned the scent of blood in the water.

The lessons my patient eldest brother taught long ago made clear a simple rule; if you have not identified the mark within thirty minutes of sitting at the table, you are it. And in short order, it became clear the game was indeed filled with wealthy players of limited expertise.

Unfortunately, when the gainfully employed amateurs broke it up early Sunday evening, I found myself reduced to case cash. For despite a run of loose play and a relative feeding frenzy for those more skilled, I also walked away a loser.

After less than a weekend in the miserable cold of another prairie town, my prospects looked grim.

But it often seems fortune prefers to smile upon me, and the men who spent the days parting me from my working capital soon unveiled a plan for my future. With little in the way of prospects and despite my concerns, just then there was little I could do but agree. Because, and due to my brother's supposed soft touch of a weekly game, a little of his kindness would be needed to keep me off the street.

As on arrival, I was again a bachelor.

It would turn out the game was little more than part of a greater plan, but as intended, I learned that much later. Meantime, next afternoon at my brother's west end storefront I turned up for a routine weekly meeting conducted in an open boardroom space behind the retail store. In those days, the direct sales outfit held such cattle calls at offices worldwide, and unknown to me, my brother then functioned as an area branch manager. The pleasant, but ruthless, fellow hosting the weekend poker game that broke me, proved none other than a regional vice president to whom my brother reported.

And just as one look shows I am not a man who likes missing a meal, games based on numbers have always seemed easiest for me to understand.

14

We traveled as a crew. In a late-model extended wheelbase van towing a covered six-by-twelve-foot trailer leased by the company. We used teams of at least eight. And from branch offices across the sprawling city, each Monday morning, after meetings held in storefronts, backrooms or boardrooms, similar vans departed.

They headed for places picked ahead of time.

No matter the city hood or regional town targeted, the trailers would first be packed from floorboard-to-ceiling with new stock. All of it, ready for direct sale to customers. Those in the sales crews would spend the daylight hours working locally. And as much as a week on area road trips, walking from door-to-door in search of people needing the new vacuum cleaners.

And what I will say about it is this; most men will do what it takes to survive.

But the pickings were often good enough to keep it interesting among new recruits, and we made a habit of taking advantage of them. For my brother made me his assistant manager. Shortly after conspiring with the vice president to prop up my entry to the business.

With first-day sales commissions of fifteen-hundred dollars.

Again, by then, I should have known better.

As a result of my bullshit place in the company, when not driving one or the other of us could keep a game running in the back of the van. While we went from the capitol to one of various towns within a few hours distance. Often, by the time we landed at semi-urban outposts such as Whitecourt, Hinton, or Grande Prairie on the looming Boreal's ragged edge, the crew would be close to broke.

Thus, made desperate, they would also be highly motivated salespeople, no matter the resistance later encountered.

I will not deny the metaphor of a snake eating its tail.

And though I recall few of them in detail, most were good eggs. But vanishing few turned out effective salespeople. Because like any other mining operation, the occasional gem turns up only after crushing many tons of near useless ore.

That is also how I met the future banker.

He was barely out of school, having earned a Bachelor of Commerce degree. With family connections at one of Canada's major chartered banks, he awaited appointment to a career post suited to a Dean's List graduate. Desperate to gain life experience and bored without school to impede his desire for action outside the norm, a curious nature led him to answer the help wanted ad running in a local newspaper. While reported second-hand, the info came from the horse's mouth a few months after he joined our traveling circus.

And though a good enough poker player, he would prove less suited for direct sales.

He was a reed of a fellow, taller than average with the usual colonial Caucasian blue eyes and a mop of high-priced dark hair. The suit he wore to the event may have been worth more than the net of his fellow trainees. Born to money, his walks on the wild side were informed by an innate caution most often found in men of similar placing.

Long ago, he had been taught the virtue of letting others dirty their hands while he focused on managing the proceeds of their effort.

We could not have been more different, but as far as employees went, it turned out he was a safer bet than pocket aces for me.

And though not much for closing sales, his good humor and smooth charm with salespeople and customers alike raised him. In what seemed no time, he grew into my right-hand man. But a single memory reminds me of him to this day, as at this writing we have not seen one another in many a year.

"Why don't you come back later," she said, "without your partner."

Just then, I was kneeling on the carpeted living room floor of a Southside Edmonton home with a vacuum cleaner deconstructed around me, making a usual show of the system's trademark efficiency.

The gig relied most on the gift of gab. Which years of teenaged girl-talk and poker table patter had by then refined into something like cool milk poured across smooth-stretched silk.

Less than thirty minutes earlier, the lady of the house, mid-fifties but well-maintained and wearing a knee-length summer skirt, had granted entrance to me and the future banker. For the product demo. She now moved from the sofa to seat herself on an ottoman not three feet in front of me, and spreading her legs revealed a prurient desire.

"My husband is away," she said, "and I could use some company while deciding how many of these things to purchase."

Her voice was soft, more than a murmur but barely above ambient.

The future banker, watching the show as part of his training, had stepped out to take a piss as I recall it now, leaving us alone in the room. I will not deny that her display moved me, and near at once neither his training nor the product seemed a concern.

"I'm through at six," I said, "does that work for you?"

Following her lead, I kept my voice low.

With a smile betraying relief, she nodded.

She then stood and grasping the back of my head pushed herself gently against me before lowering her skirt and turning away to return to the distant sofa. I recall a fresh-washed but intoxicating scent, and it does not take a note to remember the wave of blinding lust that near overwhelmed me.

Only a few seconds later the banker returned from his break, and I went back to droning product info. Despite what seemed a thorough effort, the answer was no sale. I packed up the product cases and soon departed.

After making a less than usual closing attempt.

I should also admit, the show threw me off my sales game. For the rest of that day whenever I could get beyond a customer's front door the demo that followed was worthless. I remember it turning out a rare shift with zero sales closed.

Before going our own ways at the end of it, the banker noted my poor results. And rightly voiced his concern.

"Are you ok?" he said, "I don't want to sound like a jerk, boss, but you've been off your game today."

I recall frowning, unsure of what to tell him. And not being certain of anything aside from where I wanted to be at six o'clock.

"Just a bad one," I said, "best not to worry about it."

He nodded.

"That's the first time I've seen you blanked."

I had not thought of it, but he was right. Since the setups of my first day in the field, not one had passed without at least a single sale. On most days, there were several direct sales recorded and one or two more closed on behalf of team members. A long streak of good luck had earlier broken. But in the moment, I barely noticed. And paid little heed when he pointed it out.

"Tomorrow's another day," I said, "and we'll get them then. So, rest up and I'll see you here bright and early."

With that, I clapped him on the back and made for the door.

After the regular sales team meeting the next morning, he came with me on a return trip to the scene of the previous day's closing failure. Once there, we dropped off new systems for each of that lady's four grown children. Before thanking her and soon leaving.

As the product is known for quality, I have not again seen her.

But once in a long while, I wonder what became of that banker.

15

The persistent ring of a telephone woke me in the middle of an April night. It was already weeks into the month and much too late to be a prank. I heard the muffled voice of my eldest brother in the apartment's distant living room. A few moments later he knocked with uncommon urgency upon the closed bedroom door where I lay, not alone but now filled with creeping dread.

For as my darling mother liked to say, no good happens after midnight.

And despite the common mistake, I will ever believe the traveling gene passed down to me from her. For unlike my father's early war-driven travels which gave way to life anchored upon a solitary and isolated shore when he returned, her life would prove something of a monument to movement. As a result, most times it was her tracks I would cross in later roaming. Nor will I deny there was some comfort taken from knowing my mother had passed through a place before me.

No matter how long ago it might have been.

With separation wreaking its usual havoc, however, the children first suffered the routine damage of their broken home. For despite loving them more than life itself, no matter how she tried they could not be saved from the dirty business. And while I was too young to understand, losing custody of us would come near enough to killing her. No greater lesson of perseverance would I witness than her struggle to survive as a middle-aged woman in a twentieth century man's world.

Though as she said little, it remains the story I can least surely tell.

What I could later find out, from herself and others, went something like this. One fall morning, not long after breakfast but also not yet time for lunch, she made up her mind. While enjoying another shit sandwich of a day, with neither husband nor children upon whom to shower the affection that relieved it.

My mother would make her first try at a geographic cure. Ever responsible, she first gave two weeks' notice to the pet food canning factory. Where she then worked the midnight shift on a production line.

And while an initial sortie of the holiday variety, it was far from her first adventure.

After all, at the tender age of seventeen she married the man who separated her from education and family. To extend a hereditary line and care for his needs at the expense of her dreams. Her next years were spent in the Manitoba wilderness. Consumed by seven-day weeks spent working from sunup until long after dark. Aside from her children, those years left her with little to show but heartbreak and a penniless future.

But she was also sure of the power of hard work.

And shared the gospel of it with her children.

As she said nothing about it to me, I am not even sure if she knew the bug lived within her. But forced parting from her kids would reveal a love for the freedom of travel and life as a stranger among her fellows. So, when the first long summer without them ended, while staring at another winter of icebound heartache, she decided instead to leave in search of whatever waited for her in the unknown world.

Because of school, I would remain ignorant of whatever it was she would find or even that she was seeking anything other than life as we had earlier known it. I knew little of marriage then but did not ever speak of my parent's troubles. Which were obvious by the time I reached school age, to either relatives or anyone else as I recall.

The raised voices of late-night arguments most often fueled by booze, which after years of fighting she had given up and joined him in abusing, soon became routine. To find them passed out in various stages of undress on mornings after, often still entangled from lovemaking after one of countless drunken brawls, we accepted as normal.

After those fights ended and they split up, all I can remember is missing the terror. And aching to wake up and find them lying together on a tear-stained floor.

16

Ask any who have done it and they will likely agree, the drive west from Alberta through the Rocky Mountain passes can be tricky in springtime. But even in those days, carrying any type of weapon aside from a hunting rifle as checked baggage onto a commercial aircraft could prove far more of a challenge. So, despite April weather and mountain road conditions, at the time there seemed little choice for us but driving.

And though I may have had worse passengers than my eldest brother in my time, they have been few enough that I would be forced to think awhile before recalling them by name.

He seemed near unable to sit still when not at the wheel. Instead, when riding shotgun, the various controls, and switches common to an automobile dashboard were fair game for compulsive interaction. Time and again, his fingers worked the nobs and sliders controlling the windows, fan, air conditioner and defroster controls.

I am not sure why, but the constant fidgeting made me crazy.

"I was listening to that tune," I said.

Bored with running his passenger-side power window up and down, he now turned to working the radio's dial.

"Were you?"

The surprise seemed genuine.

"Well," I said, "I was hoping to, anyway."

As usual, he ignored the sarcasm.

"Do you want me to go back?"

He went on scrolling stations while speaking, barely pausing when the odd signal scratched its way into the rented sedan.

"I doubt you'll find it now," I said, "not much radio up here for the next while."

Instead of a reply, this time I heard him grunt. With no sign of stopping, the radio scrolling continued next to me.

"Don't you have any tapes in here?"

Now he dug into the console between us. Which, as usual, was filled only with paperwork including rental and insurance papers.

"Look in the gym bag on the back seat," I said, "there's a few CDs in there, Gramps."

A moment later he sat with the zippered nylon satchel open on his lap, rummaging through its contents.

"Where the hell did your taste in music come from?" he said, "I've never even heard of most of this crap!"

I remember the remark brought a smile to my face. He grew up on early rockabilly and old country and had neither time nor taste for other styles of music. Despite the short notice, I knew it well.

"There's a few Moldies in there," I said, "dig a little deeper, you'll find what you like."

The rustle of hard plastic CD cases went on a while longer before he selected a favorite and poked it into the dash-mounted player. A moment later, one of the long dead greats wailed the countrified blues as we rolled south into British Columbia amid the drifting grey sleet of early afternoon.

It may also be worth pointing out that his reform was long complete by then. And the job to which we now traveled plainly held no appeal. Though once, most including myself would certainly choose not to meet him on such an errand if given a choice. But good living and passing time change a man in ways he cannot imagine, and my brother was not happy to be where we found ourselves just then.

And in case you are wondering, neither was I.

Because soft living makes short work of the hard edge gained only through years of focused training, and by then both of us were enjoying the taste of it. From expensive restaurants to tailored suits, signs of age's demand for increasing comfort were already too clear for either of us to bother denying. And as usual, when money comes easy, trouble seems far enough away to no longer be a real concern.

"Do not ever point it," he said, "unless you're ready to kill what you're aiming at."

I nodded at my father, encoding the cherished words in memory gilded by a seven-year-old's pride with a metaphorical chisel. The first day shooting had been a success, and I recall pride threatened to burst my chest.

In long ago wartime army days, he qualified for sniper training.

That info came not from the man, but the many neighbors and friends who went through the conflict with him. Often, when they drank or hunted together, I would hear his prowess with a gun praised by them. And wonder at the source of their respect. But like most unfortunate enough to experience it as a soldiering participant, he said nothing about either the long-ago war or what part he may have played in it.

He could certainly shoot better than anyone I have seen. And I am not sure about this, but his goal in teaching me the skill was likely to relieve himself of my over eager and near constant harassment. Because like most any other of western Canada's many farm kids of the day, I wanted to hunt and kill with the men. And hoped to share the pride and comradery that seemed earned only by doing it.

The lessons took far longer to complete and proved harder than

I imagined. As they taught him in the service, my schooling began with safety training, followed by learning to take apart and reassemble a rifle from start to finish. Next, the cleaning and maintaining of a weapon upon whom one's life and well-being most usually relied, was studied. And every lesson must be completed in triplicate before the student could move on to the next. When the day finally came for me to first squeeze a trigger, an unnatural act felt close to an instinct.

I recall him smiling as he looked over my first groupings, tightly spaced with a twenty-two-caliber rifle through open sights. Though far from sentimental, his pride at my show of skill beyond the usual beginner was plain.

"That's good shooting," he said.

I remember a feeling like I then thought soaring must be, lifting me like a bird in flight. And for a too short moment, basking in the unaccustomed warmth of his hard-earned praise and rare affection.

So far as I know, poor country folk have always hunted for their daily bread.

Despite the short hunting seasons placed on local game animals by a distant government, for us it was a year-round job. We needed the game to survive. Even before the shooting lessons began, I would go hunting my father for a couple of years unarmed.

Each time, he taught me the skills of tracking, using the wind, building, or finding cover. Along with countless other meticulous habits necessary to the successful hunting, killing, and preparing of wildlife. For us to later eat. In those early days, though my stomach turned whenever making close contact with the dead, my life seemed like it must be about the greatest adventure a boy could have.

As I would someday learn, however, for many there is no joy found killing. But given the terms under which the world did business, it seemed best to keep that info to myself.

17

And what I said before about how physical degradation wrought by passaging time usually fools those living through it should be no surprise to anyone by now. A one-time high school student and thus at least somewhat familiar with history, I cannot explain why it so routinely makes an ass of me.

Already a few years into the habit of living well by then, neither my elder brother nor myself were in the shape necessary to life on the street. I was sure of it, and though the question went unasked, also near certain big brother felt the same. Still, there is likely no way he would have agreed to my packing the iron, and for that reason I did not tell him about it.

Because, knowing the people with whom our sister competed for business, I had no desire to be among them unarmed.

And it bears a repeat. My first choice has always been to not resort to violence when handling trouble in business. For in my experience, going beyond parley and redress does little good for anyone. While costing everyone time and money.

But failing to plan means planning to fail.

And once upon a time neither of us made a habit of walking into a joint without one. So, while I did not ask about his, my strategy was based on keeping me alive. Along with my brother and sister, if possible.

Whatever the price, at the time I believed myself ready to pay it.

As a result, concern now sat in the back of my head like a cancer, growing limbs and extending its reach with the passing miles. And much as a lifetime of systemic racism produces the high blood pressure that kills so many of Canada's Indigenous peoples, it sickened me.

I had not spoken to her since departing the lower mainland a couple of years earlier and had no idea what might have taken place. In the night, my brother spoke only the cryptic few words needed to raise me from the warm shared bed in which I had been sleeping.

"Get up, bud," he said, "Sister needs us on the coast, it's urgent."

Without a question, I rolled from between the sheets. And began readying for our high-speed journey across the foothills and between the snow-capped peaks. Due most to the rush but partly to underlying dread, I had not yet bothered to ask what specific emergency required our joint response. Much as I wanted to, the closer we drew to Vancouver the more pointless asking seemed.

After all, no matter the reason, it is not like I would have refused.

For despite broken homes regularly scarring branches of the extended tree, to this day family remains first with me. As far as I know, it is roughly the same with everyone else in our generally unfriendly and mostly dissociative clan. Which is to say, if you pick a fight with one, you have unknowingly declared war against the bunch.

And should you reach for a picket, any clash must certainly escalate at lightning speed from there.

I dropped my brother at a local car rental agency. On the way back to our leased four-plex apartment in the Westend, I first stopped into the Southside home of the now trusted regional Veep.

From there, minutes later I headed for the local racetrack. When I got there, a groom known to the Veep met with me in the corner of a parking lot. After swapping hellos, he handed me a paper bag holding what I hoped most not to need in exchange for a crisp pair of Canada's then brown c-notes.

A moment later I was on my way, and thankfully, have not seen the fellow again.

Because this call for reinforcement was but a latest. And though help was the only favor asked so far, trouble often seemed to follow when the request came by cryptic phone call in the sleeping middle of a peaceful night. I recall thinking about that off and on through the long day of travel but said nothing of it to my eldest brother.

Instead, we argued over the relative merits of popular music created by his generation versus that of mine. Like most such talks, though it neither changed a mind nor made a fan of either of us it helped pass time that seemed to crawl no matter how fast I drove.

He complained about my driving, which was another habit. Similar empty chat, a practice when sharing pressure, continued through that day. With topics growing more vacuous the farther we traveled, it seemed anything was better than talking about what we might find upon making it to Vancouver.

And maybe because I did not ask, he did not tell. But it was plain my brother was worried about whatever waited for us at the end of our journey. Though he offered no details through a twelve-hour drive into the heart of British Columbia's over-populated lower mainland.

18

What my mom told me was this.

"If you haven't got something nice to say," she said, "keep your mouth shut."

I do not know about you, but even as an adult such guidance from a parent, no matter how unwelcome, was taken without reply. And being told was not only a chance to avoid a slap in the mouth, but near as often a show of love.

By now, I have long forgotten what smart-assed remark might have prompted her saying it the first time. But she would find cause to repeat the phrase often enough to make it impossible for me to forget.

And, despite a regular urge to do otherwise, I would somehow make a habit of following her decree. Thus, at least so far as I am concerned, it is one of few redemptive virtues found in these parts.

And while there is little cash value in it, I remain grateful to my mother for instilling the priceless knowledge.

So, maybe that explains why I prefer listening. For reasons unknown to me, it seems the habit was picked up in childhood. As a result, despite my best efforts to avoid them since, I have always been a sucker for a tall tale. And much like a child, the more fantastic a story, the greater pleasure that is eventually derived from hearing it.

When my sister might have been fifteen and I perhaps as old as eight, she started me on a search for answers. That would someday lead to what I now understand as intellectual freedom. It was not intended of course, but the results might even justify the ridiculous means.

What I know for sure is, though mystifying in the moment, I have since been grateful to her for the schooling.

Anyway, before I start with this part, it is likely best if I point out that for me, awakenings are pretty much confined to getting out of bed in the morning. Despite this, I spring from a family long trapped in the mental and emotional gyre of what is a widely believed need to most in the clan, spiritual redemption via organized religion.

With my sister, as a teen she would buy into a fantasy sold by a local troupe of hippified 'holy rollers'. That shared but another example among the dizzying array of choices available to a postmodern believer at that time.

And while the memory is dim, it seemed everyone in the extended clan was finding the g-o-d in those days. Though what seems clear now is that all of it was less so then. There were also a few untimely deaths in both close and extended family at about the same time. Later, I would assign the mass conversions to a kind of community-wide hysteria.

But no matter their source, the lessons would later prove their worth.

And despite the pretty big age difference, my sister and I were tight as kids. When my parents split, she took over the role of mother to the younger children. In time, she would also grow into advisor to elder cousins and then de facto leader of a gang selling sex and drugs.

But that was later, and I am not trying to claim either as results of the other. What I most recall is, through those first months after our folks split, she always seemed willing to make time for me.

So, it was not like she had to drag me along on the first Sunday I recall going to that funky service, because I pretty much begged to go with her. And let me tell you, it was a production unlike anything I had so far seen. When thinking of the performance now, there is little wonder at why she was taken in by it. Because, though I had no real idea what they were talking about, the dancing, singing, and carrying on looked to be great fun. Besides that, from where I sat watching the show, my sister appeared to have the time of her life. And even then, seeing her happy brought me great joy.

Whereas now, much like the surreal leftovers of a hallucinogenic dream, I recollect only a few of the most unfortunate details.

A long-haired and heavily bearded Caucasian fellow, youngish and wearing a ragged tie-dyed poncho and faded blue jeans led the revival-themed show. On filthy bare feet he wore leather sandals as he read from a text claimed to be a New Testament. The timbre of his voice was that of the old-time revival preachers I had seen in those black-and-white movies on TV.

And much like a folk singer then on the radio, he sold a desperate gospel that encouraged revolution. While serving discontent in an ugly but unique voice.

That revealed nothing, either new or helpful, to anyone who listened.

The would-be preacher was joined on stage by a cavalcade of friends. Made up of earnest touch healers and acoustic guitar equipped singers with long hair. Plus, a semi-nude choir that harmonized off key, but did so with a crazed gusto.

Taken as one, I recall it as a fun, but plainly amateur, show. That was barely enjoyed as a religious appeal by my childhood self. Looking back now, I can only wonder if that is what made them seem so much like homegrown messiahs. If only to an aimless and privileged generation.

Sadly, for them and those that have since followed, and much like countless earlier saviors, the new shepherds would lead no flocks to any promised lands.

I am no longer sure why, but after going to the first show I tagged along with her for more of the same. So, the following week, I again asked to attend. For the next few Sundays, it became our habit to attend the ragged sermons together. And no matter what life was dealing, I still remember the way she smiled after attending what even my childhood-self soon believed to be foolish weekly gatherings.

Within a couple of months however, serious discomfort with the goings on at the 'new' church made a home in me. Maybe it was seeing people babbling, supposedly under the guidance of a 'heavenly spirit,' that turned me off. What I know is this, the sight of my sister swaying and mumbling under the weight of that unkempt congregation's passion unnerved me.

I recall the boyhood version of myself wanting to run away more than once.

But he was too scared to leave his sister alone with that creepily entranced group of hairy beggars.

And when at last told I no longer wanted to attend the service, my sister's sorrow was impossible to hide. She at once set about convincing me the choice was folly. We spent several lengthy afternoons together, locked in metaphysical contemplation. That was far beyond my brain's pay grade at the time. As like any good soldier, my sister was prepared to fight for her baby brother's mortal soul. The lengthy and mostly forgotten talks proved not only largely over my head, but powerless to change my mind.

And to this day, I am grateful to her for opening my eyes.

19

It was one of a host of intros my sister would give me. Among them I also count my first fix, sex worker, and transsexual person. Because as I later found out, it turned out religion, new or old, did not turn the trick for what ailed her either.

And though I did not know it when the search began, seeking my first shot of smack would lead to a Higgins Avenue drag bar on Winnipeg's low track prostitution corridor.

Wasted and unaware of who surrounded me or what I might find there, my sister showed up like an unwelcome ghost among the mirror ball reflections of a crowded dance floor. Already too far gone to register shock or surprise, I am no longer sure if days, hours, or minutes next passed in the kaleidoscope of fantasy and imagined memory that survives.

As I now recall, it was but one of many nights on which the future seemed a long-odds bet.

"Snap it out," she said, "bubbles will kill you."

I nodded, tapping my fingernail against the graduated markings of a plastic syringe. As the few remaining bubbles collected, I squeezed them out of the needle's business end along with a few drops of milky liquid.

"Well done," she said, "are you ready?"

Looking back, I can no longer remember when I first became aware that my sister was transsexual.

The knowledge seemed to come by osmosis, with her female traits accepted without question in childhood by siblings. I cannot even recall asking anyone about it. Even more surprising, my parents also said nothing to anyone either in or out of the family. Only later, maybe in puberty or because of time spent with extended family and kids at school, the troubles began.

From that point on, prejudice and bigotry took an even greater role in my sister's life than they did for the rest of us.

Because as hard as it is to believe, there remains something worse than being born Indigenous in Canada. For as a transsexual, my sister must forever navigate a world hostile to what or who she might ever want to be.

I think I remember nodding. The memory of it is much blurred now. I was seriously wired, and it was a long time ago. As by the time we met on that night, I am also near certain I had already been partying for at least a week. And while impossible to say for sure now, I might have been looking for heroin to counteract the cocaine, wildly popular and a sale item at the time, and hoping to get some sleep.

Anyway, I remember extending my arm and the transsexual hooker seated next to me, who guided my work, moving to swiftly tie it off.

My sister had earlier introduced us, in the John of that same low track hotel. Where we three shared the cocaine, which I might remember wanting to quit, from thick white lines laid out on the lid of a toilet. And much like my petite brown sister, the lean and muscular Caucasian male-to-female transsexual in transition augmented her sex trade income by selling smack.

I can no longer recall her name.

Some unknown time later, in a single room without-bath choked with dried sweat, warm lube and cheap perfume on the second floor of another dilapidated hotel, between tricks she set me up for my first time. I remember little about the resulting trip now, neither duration nor even its eventual end. And thankfully, for me, even years later the stuff seems like much ado about nothing. As to my endless good fortune, despite neither immediate ill effect nor lingering sober regret it has, so far, proved the last.

But my fondest wish on that long-ago misbegotten evening; the emotional rescue of dreamless sleep, did not show up to save me.

BLIND

20

Fallen leaves, tinged with rust and crisp underfoot, swirled around the steel-toed work boots covering Ben Thornton's sweating feet. The collar of his green coverall was turned up beneath a sheepskin lined vest zipped tight against a sharpening breeze. He hurried along the quiet street on the edge of Winnipeg's north end.

His stomach grumbled.

The dream of a hot dinner waiting stirred a quicker pace.

Now home more than a dozen years from the war, Ben smiled while looking at the neat homes lining the block on either side of him. Though a blue-collar neighborhood, still fresh memories of post-blitz London improved its appeal.

A half-hour ride on one of the newish diesel buses, a less romantic but more efficient replacement for the electrified streetcars, left only a two-block walk. To the rented three-bedroom walk-up version of urban paradise where his loving wife and their four kids waited to greet him. The work he did, hard, and dangerous unless compared to combat, was a small price to pay for their happiness.

Besides that, other than farming or fishing it was near impossible to make a living on the reserve in the years after the Second World War. Ben had tried both before leaving with the army for Europe and hoped to make a living by logging after it. With his wife and the first of his children in tow, he did his best to make a go in the untamed bush of the northern reserve through the end of the forties.

Now living in the city, for the last few years he worked a regular series of seasonal trades job arranged by an army buddy. Many old friends, relatives and more than a few members of his wife's family also lived at the province's capitol. With most of the men finding work at manual labor or tradesman's jobs as the world responded to rapid post-war population growth.

Though neither safe nor well-paid, Ben was grateful for the job on a crew made up mostly of relocated cousins and former comrades. Along with his Metis best friend Wes, a brother also worked beside him as they tunneled beneath the streets of the booming city. Supervised at a distance by college educated Caucasian fellows wearing white hard hats, the mainly Indigenous workmen spent their days like anthropoid moles. Often, they laughed at each other's appearance in the sweating half-dark. While the normal world carried on, cool in the sunshine, only feet above them.

On most days, sweating in the musty darkness, Ben recalled a cabin near one bank of the Fisher River where he and his wife spent the first years of their marriage. Made of logs carved by his own hands, winter mornings next to the frozen river were cold. Until the pot-bellied black tin heater turned red from the tamarack rounds blazing inside of it.

Mary would build fires in both stoves before crawling back into bed to warm up and wait for the kettle to boil. She would not light the coal-oil lamp on the kitchen table until later, when getting up to make the coffee and start breakfast. Ben smiled as he recalled making their kids on a rope-sprung bed in the two-room cabin. With the first baby sleeping next to them in a bunk hung from its moss-chinked wall.

And while there could be no denying steam heat and electric light eased the daily lives of his family, Ben often missed warming up with Mary on those chilly mornings. As if on cue, the fall wind at his back, blowing a storm from the distant arctic, pushed him onward.

When the apartment appeared on the corner of the next block, a grin spread across his handsome brown face. Again, he stepped a little faster.

21

The battered alarm clock, placed in the middle of a low table next to a single bed, echoed against the empty walls of a light-house-keeping room with bath. With a grunt of something that might have been disgust, Wes Paul reached out to turn it off.

For a moment, he listened to the silence. A sigh of what could have been resignation later, he rolled from thin blankets to sit on the edge of the low iron bunk. He arched his back, reached for the ceiling, and stretched. Again, he silently cursed the sagging springs of the rooming house bed.

An hour away on the crowded transit bus, work began at eight. At home, the horses would be watered and fed by now.

Once more, he asked himself the same question.

Why was it so much more difficult to get out of bed when somebody else was paying for his time?

He did not know the answer. But to Wes, it was far worse than being in the army.

At least there, he could appreciate the urgency.

The farm was like that. Everything relied on everything else to stay alive. Right in front of you and clearly dangerous. Close, so you could not forget.

The construction jobs were filled with hidden dangers, like snipers lying in wait among the ruined silence of once peaceful German villages. Wes had yet to find a single trades job he enjoyed, even a little. If not for his best friend Ben and their close-knit crew, he would be working the farm with his dad and brothers.

As usual, money made most of his life choices.

The outfit had remained together since leaving for basic training at Ontario. From there to barracks in the English countryside, through the nightmares of the Hochwald Gap and all the way to Berlin. Along with their allies they conquered what was left of Nazi Germany. He and Ben were best friends and neighbors growing up together in the Interlake district, surrounded by cousins who also signed up for the European war.

He first met Ben on a baseball diamond before grade-school. They would later anchor the reserve youth team, winning tournaments and traveling to play against other reserves and even a few Caucasian schools in the province. The tall brown kid with rare blue eyes played shortstop while the sturdy and fair-skinned Wes played second base. A close friendship grew along with their skill at turning a double play.

Ben was a year older but treated Wes like an equal.

In the service, Ben's natural leadership skills would earn him the twin stripes of a corporal despite his brown skin. The pale-skinned best friend Wes, though only a private, served as his right-hand man, helping keep their company alive through the years of war. Known in polite society today as Metis, in youth and throughout Army life he was called, sometimes affectionately, a half-breed. A seventeen-year-old boy when he signed up, Wes returned to Canada a decorated warrior, older than the twenty-one shown on his birth certificate.

The years since had proven less fulfilling for a shell-shocked bachelor and veteran.

Discharge from the service, something he found himself looking forward to with as much concern as he had combat, turned out an uneven celebration. To him and other Indigenous men returning from the fight to free Europe, the people of Canada seemed to want to forget about anything that might have happened to them over there.

Or what they might have done for their country.

And between the men, there was little desire to rehash it. What they went through back there was best left to memory. After all, it was a war, and every participant was surely guilty of something.

Much like everyone else, Wes would have to come to terms with whatever he had done in the name of freedom on his own.

22

"Sean, get your brothers cleaned up," Mary said, "your dad will be home for dinner."

She raised her voice, while turning from a steaming pot of boiled potatoes draining into the kitchen sink.

A moment later, from the living room of the five-room apartment her third child called back in reply.

"Ok, ma!"

Sean's voice was near enough to a younger version of her own.

And for unknown but much appreciated reasons, the boy seemed to be maturing ahead of his time. Unconsciously, Mary favored the child, by now often relying on him to direct the rest of her sons. Even the older boys, perhaps sensing a natural order, readily accepted Sean acting on her behalf.

The boys arrived quickly, starting the year after Ben returned from a war in Europe that now seemed a long time ago. Over eight years, four sons and scarcely a minute's rest had passed since the day her oldest showed up a month early. Mary was grateful for Sean's help around the house and gave little thought to the differences now showing up between the boy and his brothers.

She listened to the squabbling start in the living room as Sean herded them toward the apartment's lone bathroom.

The grin that spread across her face was involuntary, and she suppressed the smile as soon as she noticed it. Life in the city was good for her and the kids. But she knew providing it meant hard work for Ben, and the guilt she felt was real.

Mary enjoyed city life.

The kids, after a short time to adjust, also seemed to thrive. For their life in the country had been one of baleful squalor. They soon learned to enjoy the luxury afforded an urban resident. As the school was only a short walk from their home, Mary found she worried less about them than she had on the reserve.

And Mary too, on occasion gave way to moments of private joy.

No more carrying heavy buckets from a dangerous and untreated river water supply. No more splitting and carrying wood, rain or shine, summer, and winter, to keep fires burning around the clock so her family should not freeze to death. No more working twenty hours out of twenty-four to feed her family and ensure their survival. While her husband fought to secure little beyond the necessities from what even then seemed to her a cruel wilderness.

Often, she knew Ben was forced to risk his life, and theirs as well, in the daily struggle to earn a living.

And more. From bears, coyotes, and wolves to the wild river on which they must travel to escape the wilderness around them in event of an emergency. For her and the kids, life on the reserve meant living with danger ever nearby. On many nights, as she lay awake and listened to her family breathing in the absolute dark of the wild country around them back then, her heart filled to the brim with an unknown but sincere dread.

From not long after their marriage, the worry had been with her.

One night, some months after they moved to the third-floor apartment in the growing city's north end, Mary woke from a deep sleep. From their living room, the sound of a steam radiator burbled its warmth into the soft glow of an urban night. On the comfortable and thick mattress next to her, Ben's sleeping breath came easy as he rested from another long day of hard labor.

In a bedroom across the hall, she imagined the sound of her kids breathing. From the kitchen, she heard the fridge switch on to cool their food and keep it safe. On the bedside table, a trusted alarm clock ticked its reliable tock.

Of a sudden, Mary realized their home was warm, dry, and safe. Through the curtain a streetlight lit the sidewalk outside their apartment's outer door. Neither bears nor wolves waited in the dark to steal away or harm her children. In the far-off distance of the quiet city night, a siren called for someone else, and she was grateful.

With a start, she realized the old fear was missing.

If only she could stop time. When she did, Mary would keep them all here, safe, and happy, forever. In that moment, it was what she wanted most. Or maybe it was always what she had wanted. There in the calm dark, she could not tell.

But it was what she wanted then. And just like that, she understood.

She had listened to Ben breathing. She again wondered about sleep. Because sleep made it seem like he was not even there. It was almost like when he was away at war. Mary would pretend he was next to her then, though they had not yet shared a bed. Somehow, it seemed believing he was there with her kept him safe. At least, that is what she had told herself when he was off fighting in faraway Europe. And later, whenever he would be working, hunting, or fishing or otherwise in danger, she kept him next to her, the same way, until he physically returned.

It became her habit. To the point she forgot about doing it. After a few years, she started having talks with him in her mind. About the kids mostly, but also the usual things a person might discuss with someone close when they had returned from being away. Like what she was doing now and what she had done while he was gone. And of course, what she wanted to do with him when he got back.

Mary learned one thing better than anything else throughout

the lengthy breach caused by the foreign war; she loved Ben. And lying next to him there in the darkness of their bedroom, she had also smiled.

Because just then, it seemed she loved him even more.

23

"So," he said, "what do you think?"

The hard ball slapped into the grooved pocket of his leather glove. A spring sun warmed the green grass covered field and sparrows in the tall Poplar trees around it sang of life's endless unknown potential. Empty save for the two young friends playing on it, a faint scent of new-mown grass yet lingered in air so still it seemed to sparkle.

"I'm not sure ma will sign," Wes said.

Ben fired the ball across the empty diamond to his best friend.

"What about the old man?"

Ben circled the return toss, a faux grounder short of third base, and flipped a throw to lead Wes over the bag at second while he ran hard to cover first. With nonchalant ease, he gloved a rocket that met him as he touched the white square, anchored next to fading chalk marking a foul line, with the toe of an outstretched foot.

"Oh," Wes said, "he's fine with his boy playing hero in Europe."

He shook his head, but grinned, as he spoke.

Ben laughed as he caught his breath. For his buddy's parents, that sounded about right.

"Yes," he said, "my dad's good with me going, but ma is not thrilled."

Wes jogged easily toward the waiting covered bench next to the field. Where his double-play partner and bosom buddy now headed.

"When do the boys have the trip planned?"

The teenagers sat next to one another covered by the roof of a shed with a single wall that functioned as the town baseball field's home team dugout.

"We're leaving Monday," Ben said, "first thing."

His voice might have been tinged with regret.

Wes nodded his reply.

"I'll fake both signatures if I have to," he said.

Ben looked at his friend.

"I would too," Ben said, "if my folks wouldn't sign 'em."

Wes nodded again.

Ben knew Wes would likely do whatever it took to go. There was no way he was going to miss out on the biggest deal going on anywhere, ever, to sit around out here in the middle of nowhere doing nothing.

"I'm going," Wes said, "no matter what they say."

It seemed Wes had read his mind.

And it was also plain he meant what he said.

Ben heard a usual set in his friend's voice. Ben smiled; now sure Wes would be there on Monday morning with the rest of them. They would take the truck Big Harvey borrowed from his dad to distant Winnipeg and sign up together. After that, it was next stop Europe and the long-imagined glory of war.

He looked to their bikes, leaned against the low wooden grandstand behind the dugout. They could not ride bicycles to the far-off city. The dang war would be over and done with by the time they got there to sign up to go fight in it.

"Harvey's picking everybody up," he said, "you're second after me."

Wes smiled. Playing second to Ben had become his normal place, and he expected to earn the same spot when they entered the service. After all, following Ben's lead had worked out damned well for Wes so far. And he could foresee no reason some little old war might change that.

"They're gonna need an infield here now," Wes said, "unless somebody's staying behind."

Ben stared at the field a moment before answering.

"They'll need a starting nine."

Wes nodded again but said nothing in reply.

Then, as if sharing an unplanned communion, the boys sat a moment. With the distant hum of farming in the Manitoba summer afternoon keeping them company. And, in the warm glow of a shared faith, they recalled a game each loved with blind devotion.

The little diamond, already home to generations of aching memory and fruitless conquest, lay before them in knowing silence. It sat, implacable though scarred, unchanged in either dimension or concept. And like the game itself, indifferent to its status as the source of countless dreams yet to be played out upon it.

"I'm asking her to marry me," Ben said, "later tonight."

With a raised eyebrow, Wes turned only his head to glance at his friend.

"What?"

Wes snorted.

"Married?" he said, "You?"

Ben laughed before speaking.

"Of course," he said, "I want something to look forward to while I'm off saving the world!"

Now it was Wes laughing.

"I'm going looking for a Limey girl," he said, "unless I find a French one first, and like her better."

Ben laughed and the best friends reached out to touch their baseball gloves together, confirming the promise.

"You know it was only a matter of time for us," he said, "I mean, if she'll have me."

Ben picked at his glove, wondering again if Mary would say yes.

Wes grinned and tried to think of Ben and Mary, his best friend and his best friend's girl, as a married couple. The two of them had always seemed meant to be, to him at least, and right from the start. Without knowing why, he smiled.

"She'll say yes," he said, "you know she will."

"I hope so," Ben said, "but what do I know about women?"

Wes nodded but did not speak. Compared to him, Ben was a magnet for the girls. Not only that, but he was popular with everyone, the captain of every team and always the best player no matter the game. He was also the most accomplished athlete, the best-looking guy, and the toughest fighter all through school. As his best friend and second-best at most things, Wes often found himself the target of much reflected glory, which he learned to enjoy.

He also made the most of it.

Ben had been his best friend since shortly after they met. Going to fight in the European war was not only a shared duty, but an adventure they would only really enjoy together. No matter how their parents might feel, the friends could look after one another through the conflict and soon enough bring glory home.

And glory, even though it must be earned so far away, should later shine on all who fought for it over there. One day, maybe after they had helped save the world, they would finally receive some better treatment here at home.

24

"And here's to us!"

His voice was loud enough to be heard above the dull roar of the hotel beverage room surrounding them.

"To the starting nine of the Hodgson Flyers!"

A rough chorus of cheers followed his shout. Almost in unison, the young men drank from glasses a moment before held high. The draft beers were cold, and a first bitter sip reminded each of them of what they had done.

They were soldiers now, though not yet sharing uniforms. With the papers signed, they were sworn to do their duty by either King or country. Whatever that might be. In the morning, an army train would arrive to whisk them to remote northern Ontario for basic training. After eight weeks of misery, a terrifying ocean voyage would then lead them to real combat in distant Europe.

Even from the barroom of the men-only Winnipeg hotel beverage room, to Ben, the first sight of wartime glory was less pleasing than he hoped it might be.

"Set us up again," he said, "my good man. Same again all around and keep them coming!"

He waved an empty mug at the barkeep while shouting the order.

The man behind the bar only nodded in reply, grinning wisely as he limped to secure a supply of fresh glasses. By now, he was used to seeing the young, brown-skinned men stop in for beer or nights of drunken revelry before leaving for one of the army camps now running near full out across the country.

A childless veteran of the earlier Great War, when asked for a thought, he would offer only that the latest European conflict had so far been good for the hotel's business.

"Well boys," Ben said, "them Nazi's got trouble coming now!"

His voice was loud and betrayed a usual confidence.

The young men around him cheered again, each knowing he would make a crucial difference to the distant and unknown conflict.

"I can't wait to kill me some of them Nazi's!" Big Harvey Easton said, "there ain't no way I'm takin' shit from them sonsabitches!"

His voice was sincere, but reverent.

Unknown to the young men composing it, the starting nine of the Hodgson Flyers gathered for the last time on that night. For it was not only the end of their careers as civilian ballplayers but also their final night as a squad of only nine members. As next day, they would join the larger team making up Canada's Army. Where they would then serve as good and true members of a warrior society named for nothing less than one of the Great Lakes.

The shared search for international glory had already taken on new dimensions. And, for most of them, it would also turn out different than imagined.

Wes tossed a couple of paper bills of unknown value onto the polished wood behind him as fresh beers arrived. The middle-aged barman, with a look of what could have been exhausted subservience in the smoke-filled glare from electric lights overhead, nodded a pale version of thanks. Wes grabbed a pair of the cold mugs. A moment later, Ben winked at him but said nothing as he took one of the frosty glasses. Instead, he grinned thanks before drinking deeply from it.

Wes also drank more of the cold beer.

"That's the good stuff there," Ben said, "and thanks pard, I've got the next one."

He wiped foam from his lip with the back of a hand.

Wes laughed, feeling the beer. And something cold, like fear, settle into him as he thought of the train and leaving for Ontario in the morning.

"I can't wait," he said, "to get after those damned Nazis!"

His voice emerged as a shout.

The young Hodgson Flyers around him cheered again, a brotherhood sworn to a task and bound forever together in pursuit of just vengeance. At least, it seemed like justice, though for what none of them was quite sure.

It was there, in that moment, when for the first time Wes wondered at his intense desire to rush off to the distant war. Until then, it had seemed as much a need as anything else. But there, with the noise of the beverage room and the faces of his friends around him in the unknown city, the feelings, once so sure and backed with public bravado, seemed ready to change.

The grim weight of uncertainty gripped him. In a heartbeat, Wes was unsure of either his place or the duties that might come with it. The unknown city and the speed at which the results of so many choices seemed to pile up, now weighed upon him. They threatened his freedom and even life itself. And of a sudden, they spoke with an unknown finality that seemed to shake the ground on which he stood.

For a moment, Wes feared he might pass out.

Ben's strong hand on his shoulder near at once steadied him.

"We're going to show these white boys how to fight," he said, "you and me pard, we'll show them what warriors look like once we get over there."

Ben's voice was low in his ear, and he spoke to Wes alone.

Involuntarily, Wes turned to his best friend and grinned. He felt his confidence return as the hard resolve in Ben's tone reassured him. So long as he remembered who he was, things would be fine.

And as usual, sticking with Ben could be relied upon to make it hard to forget.

"Damn right pard," he said, "we'll show them how it's done."

Wes also kept his voice low, hoping only Ben would hear it.

The two young men, along with their bumpkin friends and teammates, were not yet old enough to legally enter the beverage room. But in that half-drunk moment of near total ignorance, they believed in the brave words. With claps on the back, they hugged and again cheered one another. Then, raising their glasses to the friends next to them, they laughed, and celebrated a coming torrent of unknown nightmares.

Because for all of them, whatever horrible result tomorrow might bring was far less important than knowing they would face it together.

25

"I'll be waiting here when you get back."

Her words lingered in the twilight between them. A prairie breeze raised a sigh from the leaves of tall trees surrounding the field laying before them.

For a long moment, Ben said nothing in reply.

In the space of his silence, Mary thought back to the talk with her mother. Not only curt, but one-sided. The future had been laid out for her in less than a sentence.

"No."

Her mother then returned her attention to the pot on the stove. A moment later, she went on, using the broken English that marked her, forever, as now a stranger in her own land.

"You're going back to the residential school with your sisters in the fall."

Her father, seated at the worn table across from Mary, spoke not a word. Instead, he drank from the cup of strong tea in front of him, clearly pleased by his wife's words.

"But mom," Mary said.

She began a practiced speech.

Her mother turned from the stove and fixed Mary with a glare that both interrupted and silenced the daughter.

"If that stupid boy survives the white man's fight," she said, "he can ask again when he gets back. Otherwise, he's just looking to slap bellies before running away from his duty, like the rest of those young fools!"

The disgust in her voice was plain.

Her father said nothing but nodded as his wife spoke, and looking at his daughter, admonished her with a glance.

Their girls knew nothing, her mother silently repeated. Mary did not know their people had once been abundant as leaves on the trees. And like her sisters, she had not been there to see what happened at the Norway House reserve. In the end, they had first begged the priests for permission, and later, help. To move their remaining people to the mosquito-infested wasteland at the mouth of the flood-prone Fisher River.

It was too late to change anything. By now, most of their people had already been dead for centuries. Not from war, as happened with distant cousins to the south. No. What happened up here came as a direct result of what the white man called peace.

For offering the hand of friendship, their peoples had been given many new and unknown diseases carried by the newcomers. Which then spread among them unopposed. And through the long years before what they called confederation; bodies of countless relatives sowed forest floors one day cleared for immigrant farmers.

How could their girls know any of that?

It was so shameful, even the white priests refused to teach it.

Befriending the white man had destroyed their society. Her daughters knew nothing of it, nor would they, if the white man had his way. Instead, from coast to coast, once free people now lived as wards of the white man's state. With all of them effectively unwelcome prisoners in a new and foreign land. About which they knew little, and in which they were not welcomed to play a part.

For their people, all that remained was the dream of survival. And many times, those dreams had seemed little more than the last wisp of fading smoke from the embers of a dying fire.

"Fighting the white man's war!"

Her mom had spit out the words.

Even to Mary, her mother's fury was clear.

A moment later, though she did not know why, Mary felt shame wash over her.

Because so far, they had barely kissed.

And even then, after she had let him kiss her and touch her a little the first time, guilt had threatened to overwhelm her. Lucky for her, younger sister Bonnie revealed she had kissed Ben's best friend Wes before Mary's turn at confession. The brutality of her sister's punishment convinced Mary to keep silent.

The residential school, despite being operated by the Catholic church, was as close to living in purgatory as anything Mary could imagine.

But that was not why she wanted to be with Ben. He was everything to her. For the last two summers now, she had not looked forward to coming home from the hated school to see her family or be free. She instead looked forward to seeing Ben.

This year, she had turned fourteen. And many times, while growing up she heard the story of her mother and father marrying at the same age she and Ben were now. Things seemed to have worked out well enough for them.

Again, she wondered what it was that seemed to make so many older people forget the facts of their own past lives.

Her mother would listen to no further talk of marriage from her daughter. The education Mary received at the distant residential school would grant her daughter a chance her mother's people could never have in this land now owned by the white men. For that, any sacrifice was worthwhile. And she was determined to see her daughter's make it, no matter what the girls thought they might want.

The residential schools, a policy of Canada's government continued into the nineteen-nineties, were a murderous but unavoidable fact. As a result, Indigenous parents like Mary's mom and dad had no choice. For by the terms of the Indian Act, the state forced them to send their children to the distant schools. It did not require telling parents what the children must endure at the hands of the brutish churchmen operating them.

Anyway, there was little choice other than war for Canada's first people. And the fate of Riel showed the rancorous fruit of that strategy.

Mary's parents, like near every Indigenous person left alive in North America, were now trapped on reserves spread across the country.

For governments at all levels, the practice of geographic distancing eased keeping them in the dark. And by then, allowing further assaults on their children seemed the only way to survive near certain genocide.

They could only wait. And hope a residential school education would allow their children to survive in the white man's world.

"If there's any surviving it," Ben said, "I'll come back for you."

His voice broke the falling twilight's silence.

The borrowed truck was parked beneath trees that ringed the reserve treaty ground's baseball diamond, now covered by shadows but still visible from the highway. A near full moon would rise in a few minutes, but it yet hid behind the last rays of a new fallen sun.

"You have to survive it," Mary said, "because I don't think I can live without you."

Her voice was pitiful.

A moment later, she was in his arms.

Tomorrow morning, he and his friends would leave for Winnipeg and not long after that join the far-off war in unknown Europe. It was nothing but a collection of names on a map to her. Mary was also sure Canada would be less than that to the people over there. She did not want to lose Ben to a war between people she did not know. And with whom, as far as she knew, she had no quarrel.

If he was looking for a fight, there were plenty of people here at home deserving of it, and that was for sure.

The only trouble was, there were so many deserving targets in Canada, she would not even know where to start. Should the cruel Nuns be the first to get pay back? Or were the evil Priests and leaders of the church more deserving of the first shot? Maybe it should instead be the English colonial usurpers who now lived as their masters? Or would the embittered French be a better choice? It seemed clear enough to Mary that the people for whom Ben would soon risk his life were often among the worst of their people's enemies here at home.

Because far more often than anyone would ever admit, from coast to coast and for as long as they ran, many children did not make it home from the so-called schools.

And to this day, neither trial nor justice for thousands of long hidden deaths, from either government owners or church operators, appears in Canada's historic record.

It seemed crazy to her, even dangerously so.

The young Indigenous men from across the country signed up to fight on behalf of the same people who had conquered, enslaved, and now often murdered them. With absolute freedom here at home.

Years later, their leaders would deny blame despite widespread public knowledge.

She wondered how Riel and Poundmaker might feel about the sons of their nations giving their lives to preserve the white man's order overseas.

In the silent night, with Ben's strong arms around her, Mary cried for them all.

26

Wes pushed between a pair of 'C' Company privates leaning over the rail, and without a word emptied what remained of his breakfast into the rolling sea. Spray from the swells sickening him cooled the few seconds before another round of retching began. In the space separating the bouts of puking, he silently cursed the inglorious life of a soldier.

A few moments later, he wiped his mouth with the back of a hand before slumping onto the lashed crate of rations upon which sat an unwell best friend. Ben was a Corporal now, but like most every recruit in the regiment, a first sea voyage soon reduced his rank to that of seasick invalid.

As it had pretty much every day since arriving at the Ontario camp for Basic Training, staying alive while serving in the Canadian Army was proving a daily challenge for the onetime starting nine.

The adventure began with much good cheer.

When to their great pleasure, an error chalked up to an unknown clerk led to group assignment with the motorized infantry of a regiment named after a Great Lake. Which, along with many unknown daughters of long-dead British royalty, in some cases adorn the armed forces in Canada to this day.

The boys would support Canada's ill-equipped battle tanks.

From quiet English countryside to the chaotic beaches of Normandy.

Onward until freeing the French.

Only when battle-tested would they face a ruthless meat-grinder waiting for them in a place of misery and death known as the Hochwald Forest.

But first, they must survive the rigors of the rugged Battle Drill training system used by Canada's Army throughout the Second World War.

And to Wes, it sure seemed like the veteran regular army non-comms running the drills were less careful with their live fire whenever it was time for 'C' Company, a unit filled with mostly Indigenous recruits, to run maneuvers.

But while the starting nine survived Battle Drill training intact, it killed a couple of young men hailing from a reserve in Saskatchewan. They were lost to live fire, which looked less than friendly to more than a few officers and recruits. When several more men, including Caucasian recruits, were wounded in similar incidents, changes to both camp leadership and training tactics were made before word of it reached the public.

For the starting nine, running into systemic and institutional racism in the forces came as no surprise. And to a man they did their best to ignore it. Because much as it was everywhere in Canada, even in armed service the color of a man's skin must surely dictate his treatment.

To the starting nine, however, life in the army meant the men of 'C' Company were subject to less than a usual helping of society's double standards.

And besides, despite the challenge of Basic Training, Battle Drill and bigotry, life on dry land turned out easier for the recruits to deal with than the constant zig zag of the massive and forever rolling troop ship. On top of the sea sickness, their convoy must also cross the open water of a wide Atlantic Ocean under constant threat of German sub attack.

A week of unbound terror for many of Canada's soldiers, the passage would cause serious mental damage to more than a few members of the regiment.

Before reaching a merciful end on distant Irish shores.

If not for the stoic Ben, who as usual kept a heroic silence despite the misery engulfing him, Wes, and several members of the starting nine might have gone off as well. But, seeing the unflinching brown granite of Ben's face, with the slight downward curve of his lower lip imitating a growl more than a grimace, they were shamed into holding fast.

As his buddy lurched to the rail and heaved, Wes smiled. No matter what they put in front of him, Ben refused to give an inch.

"And keep your f***ing heads down!" he said.

The starting nine gathered around Ben's bunk inside their Ontario barracks, with the rest of their 'C' Company platoon standing or sitting nearby. The young men, stunned by the killing of their own during the earlier live fire drill, sought the comfort of shared misery. Much as it had in his athletic career, onto Ben's wide shoulders fell the burden of leading the boys around him to victory.

Or in this case, the youngsters standing there hoped, to survival.

Almost in unison the young men, stunned by early introduction to the reality of impending warfare, nodded their heads in solemn acceptance of Ben's stern words. Amid the fright and anger following the disaster, he became their de facto platoon leader. Only later, when many lives depended on it, would the young men grasp the wisdom of their choice. And before the starting nine left Canada, he earned two stripes and built trusted relationships with company and regimental leaders that eased their time in the service.

The next morning, Ben delivered a first reminder to Wes. It would not be the last.

"Don't forget," he said, "if I don't make it, you've got to take care of Mary. I've got your word, right?"

Wes rolled his eyes before replying.

"I know, I know," he said, "and quit your worrying. You have my word and I know what I got to do."

Another live fire drill faced the platoon.

Earlier, in the dim light before morning when Wes had no time to yet wake up, Ben extracted a promise. Wes had been half asleep and agreed to the request without really hearing it, from habit. After breakfast, Ben forced him to listen while repeating the terms.

Wes was surprised but said nothing beyond agreeing in response.

For though he did not ever reveal it, he had long been jealous of Mary's choice of Ben instead of himself. In earlier times, she and her sisters had their pick of the local boys. Mary had chosen Ben without giving anyone else so much as a try.

Back then, Wes recalled wondering if it was because of the pale skin and light hair betraying his half-breed heritage.

But in short order, Wes got over any sorrow he might have felt. Because like the rest of the starting nine, he was pleased to see fortune smile on Ben. And while everyone knew vivacious Mary was special, her choice of charismatic Ben confirmed it.

Ben slumped onto the crate next to him, plainly tired from his latest round of the lingering seasickness.

"Just remember," he said, "if this tub takes a torpedo and I don't make it, you're taking care of my Mary, right?"

With the remaining contents of his stomach rising as the ship crested another passing wave's angry peak, Wes could only nod as he lurched for the rail.

27

Like it had for Canada's soldiers deployed overseas since the war began, venereal disease near at once raised hell among troops of the regiment named for a Great Lake.

For in the despair of total war, no amount of preaching on film or threats by poster could stop the rampant sex between Europe's women and Canada's soldiers. And, from merry old England to the streets of Italy, it was widespread.

As good health, army paychecks, and few rivals gave foreign soldiers their choice of female company. For either cash money or empty promises, the relief on offer was a shock for many of Canada's youngsters.

With most raised under the stubborn ignorance known as North American morals, the results, if not predictable, were soon enough plain to all.

By the time Ben and the starting nine arrived in England, army leaders had given up a system of punishment for infections and moved on to a strategy of harm reduction. With treatment taking twenty-three days in hospital, the manpower hit proved daunting. As a result, when the starting nine signed up, they issued men in the regiment condoms on the first day of basic training.

And from that day forward, they had access to an unlimited supply.

While holding the number of cases recorded by Canada's soldiers to less than twenty percent overall in England, rates approached a third in Europe.

And in a show of history repeating, barely seventy-five years later, a strategy much like it would bring an end to the so-called war on drugs. Not long after which, use of cannabis in Canada was made legal.

In the case of 'C' Company, platoon leaders including Ben demanded everyone in the unit make use of the free condoms.

"Don't forget, my life is always in your hands," he said, "and that means I need all of you in top shape and ready to hold up your end when we get back from leave!"

He stood at the front of their barracks in the English countryside. Next to a table on which sat a supply of packaged condoms and post-sexual contact cleanup kits. The kits were placed around the common spaces of barracks. And the men were now officially encouraged, though not required, to use them. For those unwilling to 'helmet up before combat,' the scorn of group shaming must be the only guard against malingering.

Though in fact, Canada's Army, by standing order, prohibited fraternizing with locals, female or otherwise.

And, as men in the service of war always have, the starting nine along with the rest of Canada's many soldiers ignored the order. As did most other men either training or fighting around them in the Europe, no matter in whose army they might serve.

His best friend Wes, of the curly hair and pleasing pale skin, quickly decided the English girls were much like catnip.

Many young women of Europe, meanwhile, could not resist the brown-skinned men from the New World. With another weekend of leave on the way, Ben made a point of again asking his men to keep themselves safe from the disease already hitting their regiment.

For the austere Ben, there was more than either foolish military point of honor or prideful selfish concern driving these demands.

Because if he happened to survive what had rapidly devolved

into the insanity of total war, there was no way he was going home to his beloved Mary carrying a filthy case of VD. Upon arriving at the remote camp outside Borden for basic training, he took a healthy supply of the rubbers. And since, from the bowls of them free to all soldiers, he made a habit of always carrying one or two of the 'French safes'.

And though he could not say why if asked, like the rest of the starting nine since joining up, he had availed himself of the services of working women at every chance. By now, Ben also believed the plentiful supply of free condoms given by the army doctors as necessary to the regiment as their rifles.

The shame he lived with because of relieving himself with them was at first considerable, but as his time in the army passed, Ben found it bothered him less. And no matter when or where, the more whores he visited at home and abroad, the less unusual a once furtive habit seemed. Throughout the regiment, the men he would rely on to stay alive engaged in the same conduct and, like himself, none of them spoke a word about the practice.

Or its morality.

Not even best friend Wes, a fellow Ben thought upright and of the highest character, had said a word about the ethics of their group's new sex habits. Wes also made countless visits to whorehouses wherever the regiment traveled. And for reasons he could not yet figure out, something about that bothered Ben.

The lingering concerns did nothing to limit Ben's own visits to many brothels throughout the war, however, nor from sharing info about local joints with the men before leave. And much like their many other new hobbies, sharing such news soon became part of established routine.

"Boys, we best stay away from that whorehouse third alley up from the Wig and Pisshole," he said, "the medics tell me there's a redhead with a case of the galloping siph working that joint and we don't want any!"

A low moan swept the room.

"A redhead you say?"

Seated on the bunk next to Ben, the question came from Wes. With a grin, his best friend and right-hand man swiveled to face the starting nine.

"Wish somebody would have told me that sooner!" he said.

Along with Ben, the barracks erupted in laughter.

28

As her shoes touched grass inside the high chicken wire of the school yard's fence, Mary stifled a laugh. In the nautical dawn, she let go of the top rail and dropped a few inches, at once kneeling to prevent a silhouette showing against the nearby highway. Mary raised a thumb to her two-year younger sister, Susan, squatted only a few feet away in the semi-darkness. Next to her, the barely seen shape of one-year older sister Bonnie waited. The girls had escaped to visit oldest sister Sharon at a Portage la Prairie hotel as night was falling, and with sunrise near must return without the nuns finding them out.

The oldest sister left the same school a year before and now readied herself for a marriage to be held at Winnipeg. Her young man, a cousin of Mary's own love Ben, would leave for basic training and the war in Europe one week after a courthouse wedding.

Which was opposed by both sets of parents. An aggressive protector throughout their lives and ever held in the highest esteem by her sisters, Sharon's romantic rebelling at once inspired the younger girls. Even more than her graduating.

To heartbroken high schooler Mary, the elder sister's outlaw marriage seemed, at the least, heroic.

And were they caught returning, the sisters risked a severe corporal punishment at the hands of the nuns. Though most times, they would not be kicked out of the school. Loss of a range of privileges would be at stake for such a crime.

If found out, a report of the offense also went to their parents.

The sisters concerned themselves least with these risks.

Their big sister needed them, and that is what counted. Besides, overnight escapes were almost routine and considered something of a tradition at the residential school. Many girls believed the nuns tacitly allowed it. In most cases, so long as it was done quietly and the girl or girls returned before the daily breakfast headcount, there was rarely a consequence.

If they knew about it, the sisters in charge seemed to mostly accept the practice. Many felt it helped to keep the peace among students. Because with the schools working as de facto prisons for the young Indigenous children rather than education facilities, even routine penalties could be severe.

At residential schools from coast to coast, caning was both a recommended and widely practiced form of discipline.

By now, like each of her sisters, Mary had taken several beatings with the flexible bamboo cane used by the heavyset but fit nun who disciplined the residents. She was known as sister Kathleen. Delivered to the backside with a girl stretched over a reinforced and padded table, also equipped with shackles for both wrists and ankles, Mary's visits with the powerful nun left her covered in bloody welts. For many of the girls subject to the burly sister's punishment, an air of sexual violence came with the vigorous assaults.

An education environment much lauded for instilling discipline, the sight of many students standing in class was common at the school.

Besides that, there was no one to whom a resident might complain. As students making trouble did not last long. Many of them were quickly relocated, probably to other schools. The girls staying behind were told nothing about it. Not only that, but few nuns seemed to know where they went when they left, and even less to care.

In the semi-darkness, Mary gritted her teeth. She loved her big sister but liked being able to sit in class. Trying not to make a sound, she linked hands with the baby sister next to her and readied to follow Bonnie along a worn path leading to the basement service entrance with its long-broken lock. From there, it was up three empty flights of the back stairs, down the hallway to the third door on the right and into their shared dorm room.

With breakfast service another couple of hours away, they might even get a few precious minutes of sleep.

Moments later, Mary pulled the blankets tight around her neck and smiled as she thought again of the big sister. The minor risk had certainly been worth it. How else to share a little of the fun of Sharon's upcoming marriage while they were stuck in this place? One day soon it would be Mary's turn, and she most wanted all the girls there with her when it happened.

For the first time in at least an hour, she thought of Ben.

Was he ok? Was he in danger? Did he miss her? Could he be thinking of her even right this minute? By now, it was pretty much common knowledge everywhere that life was hard for a soldier. Mary hoped it was less so for Ben, knowing she waited for him here. To her, it seemed she missed him more each day. Yet the longer he was gone, the easier it was to accept their parting as a necessary sacrifice, though she remained unsure why any of them were choosing to make it.

And though Mary tried her best not to think about it, the distant war's effect on life here at home often seemed remarkably unequal.

29

And then, with allies and enemies, the starting nine made war.

Despite collective terror.

Of multiple flashes, bright against a distant predawn sky. And maybe a second later, the low rumble like thunder from a far-off prairie storm. Next flinch, then crouch lower in a foxhole, forcing your body into the soil.

Because only a blink after that, hell turns up for breakfast.

Say nothing.

Survive and move out.

Everyone else waits for medics or gravediggers.

From the fractured battlefields of Europe, pastoral English countryside was soon little more than a treasured memory for the starting nine. As what they earlier thought about life was soon lost to a rush of unwelcome new knowledge.

Replaced first by the absurd madness of Juno Beach, an inferno not even Dante could have dreamed. Then, as if surviving a bullet-churned nightmare in the bloody surf of an icy saltwater barrel were not enough, hardened remnants of the Nazi Wehrmacht waited inland to make things worse.

And for the starting nine, everywhere was devastation, as death became a more usual result than life.

The long-term effect of the garrison mentality, meanwhile, meant something else. For Canada's army was, by now, top heavy with senior officers. That soon enough proved eager to show their worth to British leaders.

Much like trained dogs too long kenneled and seeking the favor of handlers upon release, they offered their sturdy recruits for dangerous attacks without concern.

The regiments were stocked by college-trained officers with little combat experience. It would prove a challenge for Ben to keep the men of his platoon alive. Most times, the mindless aggression demanded by regimental leaders, often supported by weak planning, and led by green field commanders, threw away far too many soldiers' lives for little wartime value.

And though later review of the strategy and tactics could seem almost purposely comic, few Canadian soldiers who lived through it would ever laugh.

Screaming was, eventually, accepted as normal.

Like the craters left where buildings once had stood.

Or losing the fear of tanks spewing death.

As blood, everywhere, also went unnoticed.

A constant machine-like background hum, whose source would ever be unclear. The soldiers took it as the sound of warfare, near or far, and never-ending. It came, along with an inability to properly hear anything or anyone, no matter if they might shout next to you.

Bodies separated from limbs.

Heads missing bodies.

And too often, sobbing.

Breathe a choking pink mist, just dark enough to see, filling the day-lit air.

Or shiver through seeming endless rain.

Forever crawling, bruising ribs, and scraping knees or bloodying knuckles. The intermittent dysentery chased by a bleeding fungus the men labeled trench foot. From sleeping while standing, ankle-deep in water puddled at the bottom of a foxhole.

On night watch, jerk awake, too scared to move. Wait for unseen death or discovery of dereliction. Not caring which.

And through the opaque ink of what seemed each endless night, a stench of dead and rotting flesh. That ever hung, putrid, among the anguished calls of too-slow dying wounded somewhere nearby. Pleading, always, for a savior with a bullet to end their misery.

That did not ever seem to arrive.

Forever too wet or cold for rest.

The vast despair.

And, for a first time, aching joints.

Wes climbing out of a foxhole, screaming as he stood and fired his rifle blindly while the eighty-eights pounded them among the trees that first time.

The coppery taste of rational fear and bitter anger. Mixed but not shared equally between them.

Vacant faces, staring blind at endless destruction.

Roland Thompson's eyes, bulging with shock. As the steel treads of one of Canada's tanks rolled up the catcher's back. To bury him forever on the unknown German battlefield.

And the cursing, though ever pointless, was always needed.

A hole in the ground where Sam Bird and Kenny Cook, third baseman and center fielder for the starting nine, had been. With only four booted feet to prove they once lived.

The obvious and pointless stupidity of many regimental combat orders.

Countless dead children.

Liberators raping newly freed collaborators.

Soldiers from all nations pillaging with joyful abandon.

At the side of too many roads, the unseeing eyes of countless nubile teen and pre-teen girls with dresses lifted showing their wares to passing soldiers.

Sex exchanged for chocolate or flavorless but plentiful rations.

The laughing unknown soldier, in broad daylight and much like a dog in heat, climbing off one semi-nude teenage girl before climbing onto another waiting next to her. As both girls lay on their backs atop the hood of a by-now familiar green jeep. And standing guard around it, looking on with something that might have been horny desperation, one angry sergeant leading a squad of wild-eyed young soldiers, impatient, but waiting their turn.

The many prisoners of war, often begging for someone to spare what might be left of a miserable life.

A complete indifference, growing.

Soldiers everywhere knowing society was, much like the armies in which they served, little more than a cruel joke. With everyone locked in the ruins of a bombed-out movie theatre run by an unseen but clearly insane projectionist. The film slowing down and speeding up, seemingly at random. Without concern for what might be showing on the flaming remains of the panoramic screen surrounding them.

Among the regiment, meanwhile, arose a queer satisfaction, almost sickening, that seemed the result of killing Nazis. Barely acknowledged, they would reveal it to no one outside the service. But no matter how deeply held that secret, for most, the discord made by it would not ever leave. As each feared, it might be something found only inside of him, and specific, that proved its source.

And soon enough, the men of the starting nine could no longer recall the vibrant certainty of what seemed a distant and callow youth. That paled compared to the brutal relativism unveiled by the hard realities of adulthood and war.

Where, in the dark of every heartless night, waited only more of the bottomless fear.

Then, crossing open fields without cover as daylight breaks. As their comms foul and no tanks appear for either cover or retreat. So many Nazis high and dry with hundreds of Canada's young men exposed in a wide valley.

The heavy German machine guns awaiting their dawn attack outran the brothers Louis and Stewart Sinclair. And the starting nine lost the remaining two-thirds of its fleet and powerful outfield in service to their army overlords.

Eerie laughter, persistent, but without a known source. Among the men, no wonder at exploits once thought insane.

Though easily the largest target on most any battlefield, lumbering first baseman Big Harvey suffers but minor nicks through a lengthy combat tour.

Few of the broken villages were not defended. The Germans would abandon them only after fighting bitter delays to allow their retreat. Behind the collapsing lines, both Nazi snipers and desperate traitors riddled the country.

Along with countless starving dogs.

Through lingering, senseless, terrifying nights.

Where, in uneven shadows cast by shattered buildings, soldiers with pants around their ankles could often be seen, pretending to stand guard while they were serviced. Amid the feral growls of many wounded and once domestic cats. All fighting for survival among the ruins of a nightmare.

The countless old women. Always, it seemed, begging near broken street corners.

And no matter where the soldiers traveled, standing listless beside any shred of road or street, broken men of all ages, openly weeping.

Amid the battle scarred but still picturesque and deadly villages.

Where starting pitcher Billy Hudson stood next to a rock fence beside an unknown road, grinning at Ben, before falling dead from a bullet to his forehead. Making no sound as he slumped to the cold waiting earth.

A previously unknown rage followed close by a demand for revenge.

The sweet taste of retribution. A shared quest for fire. Grenades and machine guns. Neither officers nor enlisted.

A round up. Men, women, children, old and young.

The flame throwers.

Churches and homes reduced to rubble and ash.

Respond to resistance with bullets.

A grotesque symphony.

Composed of tears and screaming.

And later, across the regiment, unspoken, but plain, relief.

Division command makes no statement. In answer to later rumors, records show no local combat ops on the dates in question. Brigade tanks bulldoze what remains. And, maybe, they erased a few villages from Canada's army maps without notice.

But the facts of combat are best left on the battlefield.

Because for more than a few officers, the latest war was a last chance to establish their personal claim to military glory. And in shadows filled by a lingering red mist among the ancient Hochwald's howitzer shattered trees, counting the price of them would include two thirds of the starting nine.

To stoic Ben, not only platoon leader but team captain, there could be nothing worse.

As usual, only when looked back on much later, and by those not present, would swift vengeance be considered unjustified.

30

Like any event involving numbers of people and travel in the mid-twentieth century on Canada's plains, a country wedding could prove a treacherous affair.

Most times, the scene is fraught with unknown danger for both player and fan. To be pulled off with success, such a panjandrum of risk and ruin relies on the impeccable timing, imperturbable character, and unflinching will of its host.

For between unpaved roads, free booze, slow dancing, and lonely young women in evening wear, as much short-term calamity can be visited upon a rural community by a local marriage as long-term happiness created by it.

The effects are also much concentrated when unleashed on the unsuspecting inhabitants of a small community like one of Canada's First Nations.

Much as it did with their white neighbors, for Indigenous people in postwar Canada the work needed for a wedding by routine fell to the women in most families. In Mary's case this would be no different.

She would thus receive plenty of help to ensure the big day was as close to perfect as four sisters could make it. Along with the proud parents and extended families of both bride and groom, many on the reserve would join them to celebrate the wedding of their safely returned local war hero and his patient young sweetheart.

The reserve endured the lengthy delay between the end of Europe's conflict and the return home of their many soldiers with stoic patience. For the shell-shocked Ben and the remaining members of the starting nine, however, a slow return home also helped soothe psyches badly chafed by combat.

And when fighting stopped and furlough arrived, in the company of Big Harvey and best friend Wes, impatient Ben tried to enjoy the remaining weeks in England. Along with the end of combat, and likely because he would soon enough be home and shortly after that married, Ben noticed his desire for whoring with his buddies dried up. Though where it had once concerned him, it now pleased Ben to think of beautiful Mary awaiting his return from the ugly war.

More than anything, Ben ached to be with her.

At home in Canada, and near graduating, Mary felt much the same, and her letters to him reflected it. And for those few remaining months, like most lovers of the time, their spare moments would be filled writing, reading, or waiting for letters to arrive by post.

Suspense seemed their most usual pastime.

Mary was there to greet him, in the company of both sets of parents, when Ben stepped off the train. As agreed by the long-separated lovebirds in earlier missives, their wait to marry would extend only a few weeks after he made it home.

Soon after getting an official copy of his honorable discharge papers from Canada's army in the mail, the joyful Ben and delighted Mary became husband and wife. In the company of fair-haired Wes at best man and with Big Harvey seconding him in the wedding party. Ben, along with the surviving members of the starting nine, wore army dress uniforms in the black and white wedding pictures.

The event would later be considered a community success.

As the happy couple's marriage seemed blessed with good fortune from the start.

Even the usual drunken revelry, which in this case lasted through the night and well into the next day with Wes and Harvey leading the charge, proved of less danger. As despite plenty of heavy drinking, there were few conflicts and no fistfights. For a change, they replaced the ordinary drama of peacetime living with a sense of warm postwar comradery that in future days was seen only at funerals.

Ben and Mary would honeymoon at distant Winnipeg.

There, by avoiding the prying eyes and family of home, they instead began married life with two weeks of romance. When a child arrived before their first anniversary, the happy couple forever looked back on that honeymoon as the last quiet times they would know together.

And for the young lovers, pursuit of their rapidly growing family's happiness at once became their primary interest.

31

"The ground's changed around here," Ben said, "can see it, even in the dark."

Beneath the rippling leaves of a mature Dutch Elm, five men sat in a rough semi-circle around him. They listened between bites of thick sandwiches and sips of still hot tea carried to the job site in heavy steel thermos bottles. As usual, Ben had taken a leadership role at the behest of men in the crew within days of arrival. By now, several years together, he was the lead hand and worked closely with a Caucasian foreman.

And despite the fellow receiving a higher pay cheque every couple of weeks, on most days Ben pitied him.

The middle-aged foreman seemed ever harried. He reported to a stone-faced group of older Caucasian fellows wearing suits and white hard hats who plainly unnerved him. On their routine visits to the trailer from where the foreman managed both job and crew, he would visibly sweat until they left.

In the rising heat of early summer, the foreman now spent much of his time enjoying the cool of the air-conditioned trailer. While also doing his best to manage the ongoing work according to the often-unreasonable demands of his bosses.

"Did you talk to the foreman?"

The question came from Big Harvey, who had been with the company since before Ben joined the crew. It was Harvey who had talked Ben into giving up life on the reserve and hiring on with the Winnipeg construction company.

A happy wife since meant an undeniably happier life for Ben

as well. His four boys, with the oldest soon enough a teen, also seemed to enjoy the city. And Mary said the schooling was better here than on the reserve. Maybe because of all that, but just as likely by long established routine, Ben responded with patient solace to his good friend.

"Yes, I did, Harvey," Ben said, "and he told me the engineers will come out for a look around the site this afternoon."

With a satisfied grin, the large but quiet fellow everyone called Big Harvey nodded, clearly not too concerned and now sure Ben would take care of it. Things had been smoother for everyone since Ben joined the crew. Harvey's grin turned into a smile as he recalled the fifty-dollar bonus showing up on his pay cheque three months after the company hired the former platoon leader and team captain. Because much as he had shown in the army, his buddy Ben had a gift for talking to white men in charge. He was better at it than any Indigenous person Harvey had ever known.

As far as Harvey was concerned, Ben was also the best damned friend a ballplayer, soldier or working man could ever want to have.

"Be careful down there," Ben said, "we don't want to risk a shutdown. The wife told me she wants new shoes for the kids next payday and I'm hoping for overtime this week."

With knowing grins exchanged, the tired men around him nodded. While they did not share his safety concerns, like Ben, all of them worked for hourly wages. And each would suffer financial harm because of a workplace accident.

To an unfortunate degree, companies of the time relied on little more than fear to ensure workplace safety.

They were in an endless race to beat deadlines agreed to by contract. Like most companies big and small during the postwar period. As a result, the outfit employing what remained of the starting nine struggled to keep a safe workplace.

Just as many do to this day.

Despite cultures devoted to forward-thinking practices.

Or promises of long-term employee satisfaction.

Because heartless demand for shareholder profits applies the pressure leading to unsafe conditions in the field.

And much as they had in Canada's army during Europe's recent war, those few Indigenous members of many companies' workforce served as 'canaries in the coal mine'. On behalf of future workplace health and safety.

For after the war, dark-skinned tradesmen soon made up an unequal portion of those killed or injured on the job.

As despite the recent conflict in which so many Indigenous men fought and died with valor on behalf of Canada, being a person of color in the white man's world remained the most dangerous job. On most days, the remaining three of the starting nine tried not to think about it.

"So," Wes said, "are we waiting for the white hats or heading back into that tunnel?"

Next to him, Ben nodded toward the battered trailer.

"Unless them sonsabitches come tell me different," Ben said, "I'm heading down as soon as I've had myself a piss."

Wes nodded, a satisfied grin appearing on his face.

"Sounds damned fine to me, pard."

Ben nodded back at him before standing.

Around him, the crew also broke up, and amid stretching and small talk prepared for their return to a long afternoon of hard physical labor. Only a moment later, after cleaning up his lunch mess and latching the metal box in which he carried it, Ben lowered his voice and spoke directly to Wes.

"You just remember your promise," Ben said, "in case anything happens to me down there."

Still seated in the cool grass, Wes raised an eyebrow and peered up at his friend, trying to gauge the level of his concern. Ben's remark had taken him off guard. Years had now passed since he made any mention of the long-ago promise.

When he spoke, Wes kept his voice down.

"Should I worry?"

He asked using the voice of a soldier.

When Ben turned to answer him, he wore the long unseen but ever relaxed and confident grin of a talented shortstop.

"Doubt it," he said, "just don't want you forgetting."

Wes nodded again, at once relieved. It was just Ben being Ben. Now and then, he liked to see if Wes was paying attention. A habit picked up on the baseball diamonds they once shared as children, it reassured Wes to know the team captain still relied on it.

Because it meant that even here, safe, and free at home, making steady money and with no one shooting at them, Ben remained on guard for all of them. No matter where they went or what they might do, it seemed he ever would be.

And though he knew it was not only unfair but a sign of lingering damage from that long-ago war, the knowledge comforted Wes.

"Don't you worry pard," he said, "no matter what happens, I've got your back."

The crew lingered among trucks and tools on their return to work. After a quick bathroom break, Ben and his cousin Andy led the way into the subterranean works that would carry the infrastructure of the growing prairie city. Along with them strode the enormous Big Harvey, as usual, basking in the uncommon joy of platoon leader and team captain Ben's reassuring company.

The remaining men on the crew had to wait for the first three to clear the ladder before starting down after them. A delay of a few moments passed before Wes moved to follow his best friend down into the dank tunnels. As he reached for the top of the ladder, a brilliant light flashed below, and it must have been reflex that caused him to jump back. A rumble like thunder shook the ground on which they stood barely a second earlier, and it threw the three men outside the tunnel off their feet. Near at once, an explosion not seen outside a distant European battlefield shook the peacetime world of Canada.

And in less than a moment, there remained only a single living member of the onetime starting nine.

32

Two weeks after Ben's funeral, he showed up at her apartment the first time. He delivered four paper sacks filled with groceries. The groceries he claimed were from the company. With hat in hand, he asked her for a shopping list so the company rep might better provide for the family's needs.

He also requested she write the size and type of shoes needed by each of her boys.

Too shocked by arrival of the gift to argue, Mary complied with his requests.

After thanking her, Wes departed without further talk.

Two weeks later, early on Friday evening, he arrived with more bags. Again surprised, yet lost in grief seeming endless, Mary said nothing beyond a single "thank you" as he placed the paper sacks on the kitchen table. Wes made no small talk and plainly took little offense at her silence.

"From the company," he said, "everything on the list is there."

He pointed to the bags.

Mary nodded and shared a wan smile, plainly embarrassed.

"I'll be going," he said.

After locking the door behind him, Mary returned to sit at the kitchen table. The tears rolled down her cheeks as she looked at the bags on the table. In one of them were shoe boxes. A moment later she was sobbing, and less than a minute after that her head was on the table as she wailed to an empty apartment.

Then, as suddenly as the tears began, they stopped. Wiping at her eyes, Mary rose and began putting dry goods into the cupboards of the apartment kitchen. Her boys should soon be home from school and despite losing their beloved father, would be hungry. The routine of making the evening meal took over, and Mary thought of little else for the next few hours.

The handsome but always respectful Wes then made a habit of dropping off groceries on every other Friday evening. And while she thanked him for the food, other than saying hello to the boys when they were home, little more than the smallest of talk took place between them during the brief visits.

After three months of taking them, Mary contacted the company about something else related to Ben's death. She also thanked the woman on the phone for the much-needed groceries.

And while she would have appreciated the compliment, the woman also told Mary the company knew nothing about any of that. On the next Friday evening when Wes dropped off more of them, Mary asked if he could stay a moment for a cup of tea.

Her children, now shell-shocked veterans of their own undeclared but never-ending war, grieved around them in the rooms of the apartment. All their lives, the boys had known the fellow bringing bags of food to them every couple of weeks as Uncle Wes. They barely noticed his routine coming and going. In the neat quiet of the little apartment, their angry wait for a call to dinner hung like a scent in the warm kitchen.

Wes sat at the table, watching her, and pretending to be comfortable, while Mary hid foodstuff in the neat cupboards before serving hot tea. She placed a small plate of homemade cookies onto the table and then took a chair across from him.

"Thank you," he said.

Mary smiled.

"You're welcome," she said.

He sipped from the cup of tea with one hand and reached for a cookie with the other, wearing the grin of a teenager.

"I know the company isn't paying for these groceries," she said.

Mary's voice was quiet, betraying no emotion.

Wes stopped chewing for about one beat, then raised both eyebrows as he continued eating the delicious cookie.

"So," Mary said, "if you're going to keep showing up around here every other Friday night, you'll be telling me what's going on now, right?"

Her voice hinted at curiosity.

Wes swallowed the last of the soft cookie and followed it with a sip of the hot tea before speaking.

"Made a promise to my best friend," he said, "sorry if I'm poor company."

Mary cocked her head, peering at the large and perhaps frightened man. He sat across from her, with something like pity on his face.

"I'm not interested in company," she said.

Wes nodded, looking straight at her, unflinching.

"Can see that," he said, "just here to help, any way I can, if you'll let me."

As he sipped again at the tea, she noticed a tear rolling down his cheek.

And just like that, she accepted it. All her pain, fear, loneliness, and misery. Everything. At once, she knew not knowing where or what or when or why was surely going to kill her if she let it. A single tear falling from the eye of the hardened killer seated across from her proved that better than anything else ever could.

With hot pain filling her eyes, she stood to prevent its fall and spoke.

"Will you stay for dinner?"

She looked at him.

He sat with his head in both hands now, hunched over while his shoulders heaved silently from the sobbing.

A lengthy moment passed before he could speak.

"I can't," he said.

His reply was a mumble.

She noticed tears hit the floor at his feet.

"The bathroom is first door on the right," she said, "if you want to clean up before eating."

He sniffled and nodded his head but did not look up.

"I don't want your boys seeing me like this," he said.

She noticed him wiping his face with a sleeve, still refusing to look up at her.

"Look at me," she said.

It was a command.

As if by rote, the soldier living inside him forced Wes to look up, eyes red and face swollen from the quiet tears.

"You're excused tonight, mister," Mary said, "but next time you're staying for dinner, is that understood?"

Wearing a face better suited to a forlorn child, Wes nodded.

33

Two years later, an unlikely couple would marry in a civil ceremony at Winnipeg's historic city hall.

Unknown to the lovebirds, the old building was slated for razing. Soon, it was replaced with an example of modern architecture. Later, it was chalked up to the rampant optimism common in western Canada at the dawn of the nineteen-sixties.

On the wind, they could hear a distant whisper of an emerging just society. And in quick order, Mary and Wes produced their first two offspring in the early years of a happy union.

But much like the economic turmoil of Canada's heavily mortgaged future, fate held other plans for the couple. They would be forced to reckon with the tragic loss of a namesake son before his first birthday.

A relentless focus on the future was needed, however, as grief for their loss must be contained because of Mary's pregnancy. Which only months later gave them a most beautiful and much-loved baby girl.

At long last, a daughter for patient Mary to love, nurture and cherish. And despite uncommon despair at the loss of their infant boy, the grateful couple must accept as heavenly repayment the gift of a second child.

Or so the priest, already much hated by Wes, told them before Wes Jr.'s funeral.

The same fellow had little to say when daughter Sara was taken by the scarlet fever before reaching her first birthday.

In the night, Mary wailed for her missing babies. Not even the boys could shield her from grief arriving with the darkness. No matter how he tried, Wes proved unable to comfort her. For long weeks, relative normalcy kept in daylight hours gave way to long nights filled with shrieking madness.

At the end of a month, notice arrived from their landlord. They soon moved out of the apartment and into a rented house. But eventually, the brutal grief associated with life in the unflinching city led them to consider moving.

With help from his willing parents, Wes bought a quarter section of land next to the reserve so Mary would be closer to her people.

At first, the geographic cure did the trick, as his wife took to life in the countryside. And, within a year of moving back home, Mary gave birth to another son. Followed barely fifteen months after that by another boy. They would prove a scrappy pair, thriving in the hardscrabble wilderness where the blended family did its best to scrape a living.

And for a time, it seemed they would live happily in the remote country despite the tragedies that brought them there.

But life, as it ever has, carries on remorseless.

Her boys grew older. And having lived through childhood's private wars with grief now suffered Canada's racial circumstance. The angry teens demanded payment for the suffering caused by a bitter and bigoted world enslaving them.

Overnight, or so it seemed to Mary, youthful rebellion was at hand. And the untamed wilderness of their country home offered little chance of recovering what the boys knew they had somehow lost without a fight.

To the outraged young men, it seemed what they wanted could only be found in the city.

Life in the country soon became untenable for everyone sharing space with them. Not even fear of their mother calmed the collective anger. Unsure of why, they made Wes a target of regular scorn, blaming him for both losing and replacing their father.

Once an idyll of warmth and comfort, their isolated home, in but a few months, became the site of another cold war.

Neither the disconsolate Mary nor the confused Wes could reach the angry teens.

When her two eldest ran away, Mary sent Wes into the city to find them. Less than a week later, they were gone again. A pattern, or so it seemed, was set. First, the boys made enough trouble at school to get themselves kicked out. Next, while their stepdad went to work, they hitchhiked off the farm and into the city to join friends and relatives. Then, a day or maybe a few later, Wes would travel to the city to recover the boys from wherever they might be.

But within weeks of reaching the age of juvenile majority, her two eldest committed urban crimes serious enough to earn jail time. The colonial justice system next shipped them to a far-off youth custody center, with hundreds of Indigenous boys in straits much like their own. Where they must serve a lengthy sentence before release.

And for Mary, visiting her boys while living at the rural home shared with Wes would prove near impossible.

Within a month of the boys going away, Mary made up her mind. And though she had not yet figured out how they should manage it, Mary knew the rest of the family must now return to the cruel city.

If not, the jailed boys would surely suffer long-term harm.

Convinced her cause was just, Mary appealed to the confused and by now frustrated Wes for help.

As required by his long ago promise and despite crushing sadness, Wes at once set about tending to Mary's needs.

34

Mary was thus a bachelor at the dawn of the nineteen-seventies and lived with her children in a central Winnipeg tenement walk-up. From a rundown Stanley Street apartment, it was a short city bus ride to the Logan Avenue canned food factory where she worked the night shift.

And from the same apartment, in earlier days she awaited the release of her two eldest sons from the jail in which they spent the final years of the last decade. One weekend per month, she spent a long Saturday traveling by regional private bus line to visit the older boys at distant Cranberry Portage. Which was home to the well-guarded penal facility where the Provincial government kept them caged.

And when at last they came home, Mary's boys, recalled as once loving and kind, spewed the anger of young men whose innocent youth had forever been lost. Much to her surprise, she found herself unable to answer many of their now pointed questions.

Because the world Mary had known, or at least believed she once knew, seemed a long way from where they now lived. Here, on every other crowded street corner, someone pitched either a new technology or an age-old scam to the increasing mass of strangers filling a city grown so large crossing it could take hours.

And like many city dwellers in those days, Mary knew few neighbors outside the apartment building in which she and the children then lived.

Her baby sister Susan lived in sin, two doors down the dingy apartment hallway, with a latest unemployed and drug dealing boyfriend. She kept an eye on the place and the kids while Mary was away at work. With the older boys at home but having trouble finding steady work and the youngest yet in school, happiness most often seemed a mirage.

And despite living apart for several years, Mary and Wes had yet to divorce. For, much as the ethereal concept of what seemed ever just out of reach happiness, neither could decide if the lengthy breakup should be permanent. Perhaps in keeping with times changing rapidly around them, they both seemed content to allow their marriage to sort itself out. Absent any kind of direct action from either of them.

Mary thought of lonely Wes as often as she recalled life with devoted Ben.

Though in either case, nostalgia often seemed a better choice than her present. Where increasing loneliness came along with the rapid growth of her children.

And, with the boys embracing lives of their own, more often than ever Mary was left at loose ends. After they left for school, through lengthy day-lit hours without work to distract and for reasons unknown to her, often unable to sleep, memory assailed her restless mind. To help her rest, older sister Sharon suggested Mary try one of the new valium tablets chased with an ounce of the sweet but pleasant brandy.

For as the boys steadily matured, the empty hours seemed to increase, passing slow but never to return.

The shiny new habit was under control as her youngest readied for the start of school.

For the powers that be of the time, however, a new decade meant cooling to the fires of youthful revolt in North America. And instead of change, the leaders of both country's answered the fears of an aging people with offers of fiscal security.

As they ever have, the people soon arranged to get what they wanted.

Unknown to distracted Mary, for her boys and most non-white people, an undeclared but endless war continued. As battle lines once drawn for peace and love were now eroded by money's jaded contentment. While age worked to placate the privileged masses. And soon, both youthful and disenfranchised found themselves locked in a guerilla conflict.

Where either success or failure produced few clear results.

And surrounded by what often seemed the vacuum of public morality, where personal ethics seemed more relative question than objective answer, Mary's lonely young men grasped for direction.

And found instead of either sustenance or comfort, a world built by older people wanting most to feed them more of the same. While the time later known as the 'Me Decade' spun onward, a surreal montage imagined by millions of blind post-impressionist painters.

Ignorant, they worked on the same canvas.

That, when complete, seemed indistinguishable from usual ideas of reality.

Meanwhile, what appeared a common angst, once believed the fear of living with knowledge of the bomb, seemed, of a sudden, gone. Too soon, however, it was replaced by rapid growth of the same tired brands of reality-denying new-age and old-time religion.

Which then displaced youthful calls for progress and change. With rapidly aging voters calling for a return to the tenets of a more stable, but racist and bigoted past.

Onward, ever onward, the ship of fool's careens.

Then, a workday much like any other dawned for Mary. It seemed no different as she went about her usual ablutions. She said goodnight to her boys and left for work as she had many times, first stopping to let Susan know she was leaving. Before walking to catch the bus only blocks from their apartment.

A warm city summer evening greeted her, and Mary thought little of it despite heat that raised sweat between her shoulders on the walk to the bus stop. Later, when stopping for lunch at the plant, damp sweat had traced a dark line down the back of her blouse to collect in the small of her back. For the low-lying southern wetlands of Manitoba are humid in summer. And without a prairie wind to cool it, the city is often overheated after long days baking under a blazing sun that seems to hang directly overhead.

While they ate, the many dark-skinned and immigrant women, some from the Caribbean and the Philippines, with Vietnamese Boat People sharing tables with Indigenous women, made their regular talk. On that night, Mary enjoyed their company. And for a change, the often-mindless job. Later that morning, as she waved goodbye to colleagues, she was surprised to find herself looked forward to coming back to it.

But in the early hours of that same average day, before she could make it back to the safety of work, her second son, named Virgil, was hospitalized because of a drug overdose that would soon kill him.

And not a week later, the same fate befell her youngest child with Ben, the boy they had christened Benjamin Jr., who was known to all as her baby.

35

Alone in the wilderness, Wes cursed his endless failure. In a too big bed purchased more for Mary's comfort than his own, on most nights he slept in fits and starts. On many others, sleep did not come at all.

Laying in the bed alone, he told himself he had done his best. Over and over, he reminded himself, it was not his fault he was not good enough. Each morning upon rising in the empty cabin, he told himself again he had kept the promise. So much as he was able, and she had let him, he had cared for Mary and the boys as he promised Ben.

At least a dozen cats whined their greeting as he entered the barn. With several of them rubbing against his ankles, Wes placed a deep pan of warmed milk and chopped oats, made earlier, and carried up for their breakfast, on the floor of the one empty stall. Two overfed and lazy dogs sat next to one another outside and kept watch as he cleaned the stable. The cats ate. Wes shoveled the manure of the two horses tied in the other stall onto a pile outside the door.

Mary belonged to the cats and their boys belonged to the dogs.

The scene reinforced his failure.

So long as Wes could recall, he had been coming up short. A day late and a dollar light was the theme song of his life. No matter what he tried, it would end in nothing better than another bitter second place finish.

Or worse.

When had the routine failure afflicting his life began?

What lay at the root of his lingering misery?

Why did he allow it to control him?

Through the long years after Mary and the kids moved back into the city without him, he had plenty of time to wonder and often did. With only himself for comfort, the unplanned return to bachelor living was also his first chance for introspection since the long-ago war.

Wes did not enjoy it.

Because alone in the silent night of the endless wild, the same reality faced him. No matter how many ways he thought about it, there could be no escaping the facts, replaying in memory. And there, in the private recesses of what was once a bright and curious mind, a harsh fact glinted, pale and cheap, like a fake diamond.

And because of it, Wes lived in shame.

Each morning, it confronted him. In red-tinged curls that ringed his Caucasian features. With pale skin that burned in the sun reflecting from a taunting mirror. And the cat's green eyes staring baleful at the half-breed miscreant in front of it.

Too brown for white folks, and too white for brown people.

That was the story of his life. No matter where or with whom, forever trying to pass for something he was not, and not ever allowed to be who he was.

Who was he?

Now, looking back at forty, Wes could no longer be sure.

Was he the cowboy known to his neighbors? Not only a family man but a veteran. Always ready to help, though keeping mostly to himself. And by now believed a well-respected member of the community.

Or was he the construction worker of his city life? Then a bachelor, the former soldier was embraced despite a penchant for drink. And a skirt chasing habit. Because of an astonishing work ethic. Plus, the indulgence of good friends made in wartime.

Maybe he was the soldier who dealt with the Department of Veteran's Affairs? The decorated private. An efficient killer, but also real polite. With a feel for taking orders. Is that what he was? The fellow who, despite one day receiving his nation's gratitude as a pension, would never feel deserving of it?

Or was he the drunken truck driver who caused the deadly accident? He tried not to think of that fellow. But there would be no forgetting the results of a booze-fueled crash. That took a pair of young lives less than a year after the European war.

Could he be a red-headed logger from the interior of British Columbia? That hard-drinking fellow broke a few hearts, but also made many friends. Despite being unwilling to share much about his past. Before vanishing without a trace.

The longer he lived alone, the more Wes thought about it.

Long years passed in a blurred line. He was no closer to an answer that pleased him when cruel news arrived from the distant city. And near at once, from treasured memory, a young baseball player known for only a short while long ago, reminded him of a promise made to a friend who had seemed to know the answer.

And like the soldier had and a friend must, Wes put aside his thoughts and picked up what seemed his latest duty. Leaving the ranch in the capable hands of a younger brother, who survived the European war by being too young to fight in it, he was soon departed.

For his word remained an inviable bond, no matter what else Wes might ever have been.

In the faraway city, Mary needed help.

As promised to Ben, the boy who should ever remain his best friend, Wes would do whatever he could to provide it.

EQUITY

36

I pulled our rented car into the crowded parking lot of a motel next to the highway outside Abbottsford in the cold half-light before dawn. By then, I had a sour belly from a day of gas station coffee, and my breath reeked of those chips that smell like sweaty socks.

Big brother arranged for the shared room before we left Edmonton. We were soon enough checked in and ensconced, next to one another, on a pair of aged twin beds. Only a few minutes after we got there, he was snoring from the sagging mattress next to the bathroom. And once I finished brushing off most of the hair coating my teeth, I set the window mounted air conditioner to max cold and rolled into my bunk. There, I pulled a threadbare synthetic blanket, festooned with a once bright floral print, tight around my neck.

Neither the racket of his sawing wood nor a shitty mattress could keep me from soon drifting off to sleep.

Where, in the place between exhausted and renewed, lies a queer realm.

Peopled by fantasy.

And claiming knowledge of philosophy sometimes glimpsed, but only rarely, by jonesing drug-addicts and long-distance travelers.

It serves as forever home of broken dreams and fruitless self-examination. Only in lurid hours lost to science do such imagined conflicts live out their surreal times. And somewhere between departure and arrival, insight of untold value might be known by either driver or druggie.

Anyway, for me, dreams have always been taken as closer to gospel than anything heard from a preacher.

On that exhausted night in a long-forgotten motel next to Highway One, I slept through a dream so vivid the difference between fantasy and reality was for a moment hard to grasp upon first waking. And if given a choice in those few seconds of sweet doubt, I am not sure to which version of it I should have returned.

As usual, uncertainty makes all the difference.

Virgil was a writer. And someday, he intended to be a great one. So, between eating dinner and going to bed after tiring days as bricklayer's apprentice, or through solo weekend nights instead of partying with friends, he wrote. I do not know from where or when he might have got the battered typewriter on which he would tap, slow but firm, while working at it. With little renown, less appreciation, and no pay. Aside from a deep calm at seeing the words appear, neat and sure, on a once blank page in front of him.

There, in a rented apartment surrounded by an obscure prairie city in the approximate middle of nowhere, as writers have since written language began, he worked alone. And finding himself trapped in a world he could neither remake nor understand, he rendered what was, is and should not ever be.

With justice and equity for all, as best he understood it.

In the company of my younger brother, I spent a summer living with the young writer when home became the sight of alcohol-fueled conflict between our parents. I would ever recall him as a fellow of quiet humor, with a light-brown skin color and longish black hair, dark-eyed with the muscularity of his older brother but more of their late father's height. Like a few siblings and several members of the extended family, he was near-sighted. And so, wore cool wire-rimmed specs that lent an air of bookish intellect to his appearance.

Though I would not witness it, he was also known for the dangerous violence of a rarely displayed temper. Because the couple of years spent in a youth detention center with his older brother had convinced him the exciting but empty life of crime was best left to others. He departed that place with a fearsome rep. And was treated with much respect by the various hard men with whom he would later mix either at home, work or on the streets.

As he pursued a tradesman's career and avoided the criminal lifestyle so common among the rest of the clan, my parents also held him in a higher regard. To them, it seemed the pairing of sobriety and devotion to his secret artist's life stood out.

During that summer living with him, what I saw continues to influence me.

Later, from memory I would recall him carrying a notebook small enough to fit in a pocket, along with the stub of a pencil. From time to time, I could see him making notes. And later, he transferred or used them as source material for whatever should eventually be spit from the writing machine. Which he moved from an upper shelf in a hall closet only after we boys went to bed.

I knew that, because late one night I snuck from a bedroom shared with my younger brother to see what the weird clackety-clack noise might be.

With caution born of experience, I crept from my bed and surveyed the apartment as I moved warily toward the hallway's distant end, which seemed source of the weird racket. Crouched next to the doorway, I peered from behind the guard of an electric stove into a spartan but clean and brightly lit kitchen.

There, older brother Virgil sat with his back to me, alone but now and then drinking from a mug on the table. Next to it sat the notebook. Along with the strange machine he occasionally stabbed with his fingers, creating the staccato rhythm that awakened me.

He was unaware of my presence and a moment later I had returned to bed, still mystified but relieved of concern and at once ready for sleep. On waking next morning, however, I asked about the machine and the noise of him using it. And like many a writer, he was first reluctant to discuss his work. But as a good and loving brother, while readying for a day of hard labor, he promised to tell us about it upon his return.

I am sure both of us boys had forgotten our older brother's promise by the time we sat together in the living room later that evening. He had put in a long day of work, made dinner for us all, and cleaned the resulting kitchen mess. But with the pair of kid brothers spellbound on a battered sofa, he stood at the center of the humble apartment's living room, reading from loose-leaf pages held with tender care in heavily calloused hands.

Awestruck and filled at once with worship for the heroic figure in the shape of an elder brother, I hoped most for his story not to end.

And even in a dream, Virgil seemed too perfect for this world. A mellifluous voice like a wave of soothing warmth seemed to envelope not only the tiny room from where he read but the entirety of an insane world beyond it. Near at once, an overwhelming desire to remain and listen, no matter what he might say, superseded the clarity of his words.

Just as suddenly, another voice arrived, both loud and clear.

"Come on, bud," it said, "let's get rolling so we can grab ourselves some breakfast. We've got a long day in front of us. Grab yourself a shower and I'll check us out. Meet you in the restaurant next door."

My eldest brother's voice bellowed reality.

In the absence of an epiphany after a dream like that, the usual result here is a slow burning anger of unknown origin upon waking. And like it did most times, even by then, spending the night on a ratty motel mattress after twelve-hours of driving left

T.F. PRUDEN

me wanting a new lower back.

37

"I'll never forget," my eldest brother said, "the look on the faces of those house dicks!"

We sat across from one another at a red Formica table in a busy chain restaurant. It shared the building with the gas station. The businesses occupied a wide lot next door to the cheap motel where we had spent what was left of the previous night. And now, aware of what lay ahead but still hesitant to face it, we instead made a little talk and drank coffee as the lower mainland bustled with industry around us.

The story raised a rueful chuckle.

"She was some pissed, alright," I said, "it's no wonder they didn't want to try dragging her out of there, eh?"

He shook his head before drinking from a cup on the table in front of him.

"Sometimes," he said, "I can't believe she made it this far."

With something welling in my throat, for a moment I had to look away. Minutes earlier, he at last revealed to me her latest troubles.

"She was always different," I said, "from the rest of us."

He laughed again, rolling slightly reddened eyes, and shaking his head.

"But that temper!"

Of course, he was right.

And despite my new misery, I could only laugh when recalling the pair of enormous hotel door men. They stood, helpless in the hallway, as her muffled anger rumbled from behind the imposing door of an expensive hotel room.

A date had gone bad. The violent argument had spilled into a stylish downtown Winnipeg hotel's eighteenth floor hallway. As a result, guests were disturbed and raised an alarm. Which brought with it the unwanted attention of hotel management.

Good sister Sharon had kept herself locked in the room through the couple of hours since. Big brother and I were called to arrange for her peaceful exit.

If memory is of any use, it may be that I was not yet legal age when the tawdry affair played out around me like scenes from a bad movie. And while a first time, it would turn out far from the last. Likewise, for the patient oldest brother, it counted as but the latest.

Because out in the world, by then, Sharon could be a handful. And it has ever been my opinion that she did her best to live up to a feisty rep. Which she had earned because of bitter and near-continuous conflict with the world around her.

For, as of this writing, and despite early twenty-first century progress, that continues to describe life for most transsexual people in Canada.

And back then, like it or not, she must live as a pioneer or die in servitude to lies wrought by a medically correctible genetic error. Because accepting the gender right to her also meant signing on to fight an undeclared war against intolerance and bigotry. For despite asking nothing more either of us or the world at large, along with transsexual people worldwide, Sharon must ever fight for the most basic of all rights, to be.

But to claim I understood any of it, or even cared most of the time, would be a lie. While it may be that I thought about it now and then, mostly it was not a concern that held a top place on my list. And while I cannot speak for anyone else, it sure did not seem to be that big a deal to anyone else in the extended family.

For most of us, she was accepted, and that was about it.

Gender and bearing, like marriage and divorce, children and stepchildren or the privilege known only by white folks, were facts to be accepted. Not philosophy looking for an argument. And the notion of punishing anyone for a health issue is foreign to people able to keep a hold on their culture.

But, when cultural identity is lost to either conflict or progress, personal survival soon replaces concern for community.

And despite TV, radio and Hollywood filling the daily news, popular music, and movies we loved with images and ideas that harmed both personal and collective psyches, many of us were loath to admit the pain it caused.

For despite its treatment of us, we understood most the need to find some place of our own within the greater society.

As a result, even for a family as far from Indigenous culture as ours, Sharon's gender was known. It was also something understood in our collective long ago. And while there remained pockets of bigotry throughout the extended clan with whom she would struggle for progress, most of her troubles came from the unknown and ignorant.

She would eventually drop out of high school rather than continue fighting for a place among the largely Caucasian student body. That seemed to delight in pointing out the vast differences between her world and theirs. The life of crime beckoned, and blessed with an enterprising spirit, she made the best of her scene.

By taking advantage of an early start to the dangerous career.

"We'll meet mom at the airport," my eldest brother said, "and we can stay with her at Auntie's place in New West tonight."

I nodded but did not reply. It had been a couple of years since I had last seen my mother, and I wished at once for a happier reunion. Then, for maybe a second, I wondered if my back was going to enjoy the change in beds.

A moment later, the flush of guilty relief arrived. And though I did not crack a smile, knowing the concealed iron would not be needed, improved that shitty day.

38

There are choices I have been fortunate not to make, and many more for which request of my personal consent has been spared. This has not left me blameless. No more than it has any who claim, because of ignorance or thoughtless but tacit approval, not to share blame for the intrigues of society's various systems.

For the cost of living in a world supposedly governed by the rule of law has ever been guilt for the action of its citizens.

In heavy mid-morning traffic, while guiding the rented sedan with needed care, I wondered most about fault. And if perhaps I was not alone in feeling I had failed at the job of being my sister's keeper. But there seemed little mood for chat about that or anything else inside the car just then. For though my eldest brother sat fidgeting as usual next to me, he was lost in musings of his own design.

As despite the shared concern then directing our lives, a previously unknown divide also seemed to lie between us. With a difference of fifteen years, so far, there had been no experience of anything like a generation gap for us to navigate. Time had passed, however, and the older men left over shared little in common with the younger ones we had once known.

On that day, for both of us, awareness of it might have arrived.

"Can't believe how much this place has grown," he said.

I nodded instead of replying, keeping my eyes on the many cars around us, all moving far too fast on narrow streets.

"When I last visited, they had an apartment in New West," he said, "it was back when they got married."

I glanced at him and might have nodded, but again did not reply, instead keeping my focus on safe navigating of the big sedan. The hospital waited at the center of too crowded Burnaby. And managing the midday traffic now seemed like it might require an engineering degree.

"I only met him a few times before they got married," he said, "but it must have been quite a love story."

I missed their Vancouver wedding due to an unplanned holiday spent at Manitoba's luxurious Headingley jail. Later, the photos revealed Amos and Sharon as a handsome couple, and I will ever regret missing the event. Though for the life of me, I can no longer recall if it might have been an unpaid fine or a drunken assault beef that landed me in the hoosegow.

I met him a couple of years into their marriage.

When they traveled to 'friendly' Manitoba for a holiday celebrated with the family. Likely because we were both struggling to stay on the wagon at the time, we hit it off.

"I needed a place to stay," he said, "after leaving rehab, eh?"

Next to him, I remember nodding.

We stood side by side on the back step of my mom's apartment, smoking cigarettes after the latest heavy holiday meal. Prepared with love by a harassed but happy mother, because of allergies, the strict 'no-smoking indoors' rule was kept at her home.

"I met Sharon there," he said, "but there was nothing going on between us."

Between drags from a filtered smoke, I remember smiling at the notion of their unusual romance born among the wreckage of recovery.

With an unseasonably warm Thanksgiving making the late afternoon temperatures bearable and a full belly, I was content to listen. And so, the brother-in-law introduced himself. The tender care and respect with which he treated my sister meant he was already held in some regard, despite having just met. Everyone in the family had raved to me about how well he treated Sharon, and happily, it proved no boast.

That man loved his wife, and he did his best to make sure she knew it.

Later, when I needed a place to stay, and they took me in, I discovered the royal treatment she received in public paled compared to their life at home together. Where he seemed a most devoted servant, tending to her needs and making near constant efforts to please.

"Can I get you another coffee, honey?"

I was in the second bedroom of an eastside Vancouver apartment. Indolent, I dozed on a mattress laid out on the floor. A mid-afternoon sun announced its presence from beneath a heavy blanket spread over the window to make a curtain. They were in the living room and maybe not aware I was doing the eavesdropping.

"I'm good Sweetness," Sharon said, "is there anything I can get for you?"

Her reply dripped honey.

From the kitchen, I heard the rattle of flatware in a drawer.

"No baby," he said, "but I'm going to make us a big breakfast, are you almost ready to eat?"

Not a moment later, my belly reminded me it was time for chow.

"I can't wait, my darling," she said.

They lived as roommates for a couple of years before getting together. A recovering dealer, after rehab he took a night job as a short-order cook instead of returning to the earlier gig. He was an old school rounder and seemed to accept her ongoing career in the sex trade as business, and entirely separate from their married life. In any case, it was something that did not ever come up between any of us.

And like a sensible person, I accepted this as a sign it must be none of my business.

39

Amos and Sharon had thus been together most of their sober lives. And much like other married people, they were also condemned to the netherworld of coupledom. Where, along with parents, grandparents and others seldom spared a thought by either young or single, they seemed to exist on a mysterious astral plane. So far as I know a place unseen by any but those living there, it seems ever separated from either unmarried friends or extended family. Where as usual, out of sight also means remaining, mostly, out of mind.

And like it will, a decade passed before I knew it.

Much as change to the lower mainland was a surprise to my eldest brother, who had not been back since the long-ago wedding, the place like the people was now strange to me. And the memories feeding my driving led me down many wrong streets. On that trip to the hospital, my ideas about their happiness during a lengthy time between visits at last seemed wrong-headed.

Anyway, it was by then too late to matter.

But according to the horse's mouth, Amos had lived a fine life as a young hustler on the streets of Montreal. He worried most about good times and cheerful dissipation. He was the middle example of three close-knit brothers and product of a broken alcoholic home. With them, he found not only company but often adventure.

Like countless young Indigenous men in cities across Canada, they turned to more serious crime after a juvenile prison system designed to break their wills could not.

When the chance to lighten their load while helping a few

friends came around, Amos needed little cheering on to swiftly take advantage of it.

His career as a dealer began at seventeen, and he was well addicted to the smack before his next birthday.

The remorseless powder would take his brothers before any of them reached thirty. After a dozen years in and out of various jails, when Amos met Sharon, he was more than ready to go straight. As luck will often have it despite the endless complaints otherwise, it turned out she was, just then, also ready for a change.

Fortunately for the lovers, nature led them down a reliable path. And on that long-ago afternoon, as he told me their story, the smile never left his face.

As far as I know, he lived out their years together not only happily heroin-free but also as merrily sober as the proverbial judge. I can say for sure that whenever I would later see the man, he seemed to wear the smile of a fellow who had got what he most wanted from life.

And while my darling sister Sharon said little about him directly, as the years went by, they spent ever more time alone together. A picture of domestic bliss uncommon to the clan was painted there, and while not often seen in public, we all knew about it.

So, when everything blew up, it was an unwelcome surprise to more people in the clan than self-absorbed me.

But that is often the way it goes with disease and the aggressive cancer afflicting Amos would take him after only a couple of years. Out of respect for his wishes, Sharon told few of the illness until needing help to care for him at their home. Together, in stoic silence they held out in the neat main floor two-bedroom suite of a three-story Burnaby walkup.

Until he at last required hospice care.

One nurse later told me that during those last months, she rarely left his bedside.

At the funeral for Amos, she seemed to manage the grief well enough. Or at least, that is what I am claiming here. Anyway, the family gathered to comfort Sharon had already begun to chafe one another by the time I left. On the tenth day of hanging around her place, it seemed past time for me to go.

"Are you going to be, ok?"

In the spare bedroom of her apartment, I had leaned over a folding cot while packing a duffle bag with fresh-laundered clothes.

"How could I not be, eh?" she said, "with all these people around here!"

I remember chuckling as I zipped the nylon bag closed and stood upright.

"I'll stay in touch," I said.

Sharon only smiled, knowing I would not.

"I mean it!" I said, "for sure, I'll call you when I get back to Alberta and we'll do a weekly one after that, ok?"

I might have been selling dope or steroids and shacked up with a photographer at Calgary when Amos passed, but my notes do not make it clear. Because in those days, though writing was less than a job but more than a hobby, it produced neither income nor respect. Anyway, what I remember is that even to me, the promise sounded hollow.

But as usual, my sister let me off the hook.

"Call me when you get back," she said, "and we'll see how long it takes to get everyone else out of here before we schedule anything, alright?"

I am almost sure we both knew it would not happen. At least, I hope we both did. We were close, as kids. But even then, it was so long ago the people we had become could scarcely remember who we once might have been.

For a moment, I remember my throat getting thick, and my eyes welling with tears.

What became of the curious teen who once led me in search of a new messiah? Where was the angry young transsexual demanding change? Who was this standing in her place? Why did I expect to know someone with whom I had shared so little time, so long ago? When did everything between us change?

In that moment, none of it made any sense. And though I hate to admit it, sitting here today, it still does not.

All that seemed clear then, and now, is this. I loved my sister. And though I certainly did not ever know her as well as I believed I once had, she remained a person to whom I felt an undeniable affection long accepted as the real kinship of siblings and family. More than anything, it was an attachment with few if any ties to either systemized logic or rational thought. Somehow, her well-being played a key role in my unconscious experience of a world in which I so selfishly lived.

And no matter how much I might want to; I will not ever know the answer to any of those questions.

40

When together alone, we siblings called him Benji. He played the guitar like it was part of his anatomy. The youngest child of my mother's first marriage, Ben Junior was also closest in age to me.

As his older siblings made little time for music, the boredom of solo performance is likely why he taught me to play. In time, my childhood memories would fill with hours spent studying his painstakingly handwritten lyric sheets so my warbled voice could better accompany him on guitar.

To this day, I recall with greatest joy how he ignored frustration while teaching me the rudiments of music and the basics of making it with voice and guitar.

A rare talent, when touring country music making uncles passed through our part of the world, they would give him lessons. On a wide variety of stringed instruments including bass, fiddle, mandolin, and acoustic guitar. And though he did his best to pass on the info to his younger brother, Benji was blessed with an impatient and hardheaded student of sadly limited musical talent.

But so long as I have a memory, I will not forget listening to him picking on a battered acoustic through lengthy summer afternoons. The youngest of the older children, he was most often left to babysit while elder siblings made trouble for our parents.

To everyone in the family, either extended or immediate, he was also known as our mom's favorite.

There were only about five or six years between us, so maybe it was nature that created the plentiful supply of common ground we seemed to share. As I was only a kid, and with neither social nor mental health workers in the area, I guess we will never know for sure. But as a tortured grade-school boy, next to my dad, brother Benji would be among the first heroes I can now recall.

And it was not just because of the music we both seemed to enjoy.

For as noted a while back, I have been considered too brown for white folks only so long as I have been judged too white for brown ones. As a result, since about the first day that memory begins around here, I have been defending myself from someone with a bone to pick over one aspect or another of my heritage.

So, for me, racism has, pretty much only, ever amounted to violence.

And living long enough to write this down is not a sign I have yet survived it. But when it mattered most, my brother Benji showed me the proper treatment for those seeking to impose the fear and ignorance of their bigotry upon his younger siblings.

His lesson left three racist high school boys in a hospital. It also landed him in the youth detention center where his elder brothers earlier marinated. Unlike them, Benji did not thrive in the degrading atmosphere that caged him through his sixteenth year. Instead, the months of confinement led to righteous anger having its way.

And from then on, bitter cynicism seemed to play a leading role in my brother's life.

I was too young to understand. Because to me, his long-awaited release from the distant jail was nothing less than a day for celebrating. But, when the tattooed and sullen young man with black hair falling past his shoulders at last returned to us, it was hard to recognize my heroic brother. And though the homecoming party was a little stiff for all who came, it seemed to cause the most unease for Benji.

Only after everyone had left and the rest of the family had gone to bed, I heard a guitar softly playing from the fire escape behind our apartment. Then, listening to his fingers sliding sure across the unseen frets, I recall thinking he must have had an instrument in the jail.

And today, I can still remember falling asleep with the joy of his music filling my heart on that long-ago night.

Anyway, less than a year after his release from the jail, he dropped out of school. He then left my mother's home to live with older brother Virgil. It was only a few months later when he hit the road with a rock band now lost to the shifting dunes of youthful memory.

For me, his chase of the crazy dream was devastating, but instructive. Benji made a choice about his life and went after it. In what to me seemed only a moment, my brother gave up everything known for whatever might be.

And even today, the notion thrills me.

Though home only a short while, he would be gone from our lives through most of that next year. On what we could only presume must be a relentless pursuit of fortune, fame, and the many opportunities skin color denied him and the rest of us in real life. And from afar, he seemed to find a rhythm he understood on the stage, making rock n' roll.

Unfortunately, I was too young to see him perform it.

But I can still recall the sudden increase in popularity after word spread around school about my brother and his band. As to my surprise, for many of my female classmates in those days, it turned out knowing someone close to a touring band was a cool thing. And I recall making up all kinds of lies about hanging out and partying with my brother and his bandmates to get the attention I wanted from them.

As the band spent much time on the road, parties happened only rarely, I assured a growing number of fair-weather friends. This also explained, conveniently, why he would not be seen more often than he was.

But much as I wanted to, like everyone else in the family, I rarely saw Benji in the last years of his life.

41

It may be that, when or if cursed with the unending awareness and unfortunate insight resulting from intelligence a hair beyond the mean, a person must first lose what is believed to be the self before they can accept the implacable nature of corporeal reality. In which we all play such a tiny and meaningless part. What seems obvious enough is, for most people, ideas of self and the nature of reality receive little thought. Beyond what they might hear from parents on the way to some type of church.

And after all, maybe the subject is better left to philosophers.

But for some of us, escaping the weight of such notions proves more than we can manage. After burying parents, husbands, children and what seemed like more family and friends than seemed possible, my mother must again deal with the unbending demand of careless life.

I cannot tell you how she survived it. Because I witnessed so little of her misery. As by the time I came along, she had already lost a family's worth of loved ones.

Only a few years later and within months of each other, two of my older brothers passed and the world I knew ceased to be.

The detachment from reality arrived of a sudden. It began with screams of anguish in the night, and later, was followed by unseeing eyes in the light of day. Treatment including hospital stays and electroshock therapy next reduced her to a vacant husk for lengthy weeks.

In return, a distant outsider taking the place of our mom visited what remained of a forever fractured home.

My dad moved into the city and for the only time I would later remember we all lived together as a family after her release from the hospital. Surrounded by kids of various ages, each wounded, angry and bitter, he rode herd over a dangerous pack.

By then a serious but functional alcoholic with a bustling ranch, he was resolute and sober, a quiet stoic, through the first year of sadness. And despite lonely misery of his own, the only stable thing known to any of us seemed his unwelcome presence in that rented north end Winnipeg house.

To varying degrees, I remember each of us relying on him for something else. Over the four months between our brother's deaths and the years after them, he gave a willing target for the gamut of raw emotion felt by those who remained. As a result, it is likely he lived the entire while in a new hell, for all his wartime knowledge of it.

I will admit, I was as unaware of his sacrifice as the 'Me Generation', which carried on the party unabated on the streets around us.

A dim memory of forgotten scandals.

Perhaps seeding later division. That, and much shouting from newsprint headlines, is about all that emerges from dreams of a jaded time.

Where sitcoms challenged assumptions and trumpeted coming change. From then dominant US broadcast TV networks.

At the same time, democracy was remade. From the people's cherished instrument of freedom into a despised weapon owned by wealth and power. While word of Banana Republics, foreign wars and state-sanctioned murder on campus fed a ravenous, and now daily, news cycle.

And the awakening people struggled with increased knowledge of their guilt.

Aside from that, memory of tight blue jeans and overfilled tube tops jiggling across a colored screen is all that remains to mark the years of a self-absorbed decade's passage. For like it always has, life beyond the personal soon reduced to a distant blur.

And much as most parents ever remain, meanwhile, my mom was pretty much a stranger to me then. Not in whole the result of her mental and emotional breakdown, but also because of my age at the time. Later, after seeing her go through what she had to, the greatest respect I would ever know should always be kept for her.

To me, there could be no blame assigned to either of my parents for what happened. There was not even a point to anger. At least, none that I could find.

Maybe in a universe of reason. Where corporeal reality could be understood using rules making objective sense. Perhaps there, some idea of fault could be found. But in this world, where bigotry and racism, inequity, ignorance, and most clearly wealth and privilege, are so madly and unjustly shared, it makes no sense to try.

Because even to a child, it seemed plain enough the pain of living might be universal. For right then, while yet too young to grasp anything beyond my own pain at losing the pair of beloved and worshipped brothers, it seemed clear that my mother took an unequal portion of the world's misery. There could be no denying it.

To live means to suffer.

Sometime later, and for reasons of her own that will ever remain unknown to me, my mom found religion.

Years had since passed. And not long after embracing the supernatural, she was, at once and complete, recovered. Somehow, faith allowed her to see in the sad facts of life's ugly reality and the often-thankless work given to her by a pitiless universe, the plans of a divine power. Soon lightened by her faith, she had since returned to school and traveled widely.

To the joy of many in the clan, our mom enjoyed quite a second act.

For a time, she knew the sweet boredom of life unbroken by family tragedy. Aside from the death of my father, with whom she remained tight but would not again cohabitate, though she also did not ever divorce.

I will admit, upon learning of my sister's fate, the first concern was for my mother's hold on sanity.

And you are free to say what you like about the so-called 'greatest generation'. But I know myself well enough, and I also understood more than a little about my parents. So, even way back when, I was bright enough to be flattered when occasional comparisons were made between my father and me. Likewise, pride was tempered by a certain knowledge if someone compared me to my mom.

Because in no uncertain terms, I lack more than the intestinal fortitude common to either of them.

Still, if you have not lived through it yet, I would bet you cannot imagine anything worse than hanging around a hospital waiting for someone you love to die. Sadly, by then my mom had been through it more times than I wanted to remember. As long years had passed and she was a somewhat shrunken version of her former self, I wondered at more than her willingness to bear the suffering. Plainly, at her age the physical effects of such a loss might be more of a concern than the emotional results of it.

Long a committed atheist, I could only laugh in bitter silence when finding myself wishing for someone to pray to on her behalf while seated in the antiseptic glare of a cold hospital waiting room. And though a pathetic excuse, I am going to my grave claiming the short-lived notion came from a desire to spare my mother pain, not cowardice.

Because like it or not, we must share another deathwatch.

42

So long as I have a memory, the antiseptic bouquet of chlorine will remind me of hot summer afternoons spent hanging around the public swimming pool at north end Winnipeg's municipal Kildonan Park.

Entry to the park was free and prices for the pool were suited to a former working-class neighborhood around it. The enormous park complex, including public golf course, popular live theatre, and plenty of open spaces, was then a favored spot for young locals seeking a tan.

In the days before widespread knowledge of either climate change or skin cancer, the practice of summer skin-darkening was common among the pale-skinned.

And the season brings lengthy hours of dazzling sunshine, extreme heat, and crazy levels of humidity. Which makes water-based fun much loved by most Manitobans. For teenagers living in the north end of Winnipeg in those days, 'K Park' had gained near mythic status as a source for summer fun and casual romance.

Despite a rapid up-scaling then pushing the value of real estate around it, the place was often packed with summer sunseekers.

Of varying backgrounds. From shortly after dawn to just before dusk, beginning in early spring and extending into late fall. And in keeping with such a legendary local hangout, many a fine Winnipeg love story has there found its spark.

For even in the scum-filled backwaters of life reserved for Canada's poor, tortured by inequity, and harassed by society's uncountable injustices, the reliable glory of nature's simple beauty serves to brighten an outlook.

Dotted with stands of mature Dutch Elm trees, the park reclined, graceful, along the northern bank of the wide Red River. It welcomed all in search of nature's charm regardless of social status. An oasis among the bustle of a growing city, open flats and rolling hills covered by lush but well-trimmed grass left no shortage of choices for either recreating or relaxing.

I would spend most of my time there enjoying the nubile female scenery.

While fancying the uncertain comfort of a towel spread on the concrete deck surrounding the pool's ever crowded depths. Often, staying prone on my belly in the blazing sunshine was the sole means of hiding my shortcomings from an unkind world. As like it or not, life during the reign of the men's bikini swimming brief left little to the imagination. And while only rarely causing problems for adult males, with teenaged boys it could often be a reason for either sensation or shame.

Though it pains me to confess it, by the time I started hanging around the public swimming pool at Kildonan Park, I had found plenty of both.

But I was far from alone in possessing a libido active at what might have been a too-early point in life. For living as we did, in a world peopled with brothers spread across near twenty years, it seemed most talk between us soon got around to the subject of girls. Not only remote to the younger boys but mysterious, as older brothers gained knowledge, they shared early reviews.

We then, inevitably, transmuted the info on the way to our dreams.

The untimely demise of the brothers closest to us in age then left me and my youngest brother cut off from our source of life's most prized info. As a result, the endless curiosity of childhood perhaps too soon gave way to an overwhelming need made worse by arrival of adolescence.

And unlike my brothers, who liked their own kind, my tastes were prejudiced. For better and worse no doubt, I wanted the white girls. And to the joy of my teenaged self, the public swimming pool at Kildonan Park served a daily buffet of north Winnipeg's best looking. There, through lengthy afternoons inviting romance, the many blonde-haired and blue-eyed offspring of post-war refugees now living in the growing neighborhood gathered.

As it turned out, my father's war had displaced many of their parents and grandparents from distant eastern Europe.

In the company of my younger brother, assorted friends, and cousins, hanging out at the park through a long summer the year after my two older brothers died was about the only escape that worked. And making empty small talk with teenaged granddaughters of the war fought by my father long ago somehow made sense.

Anyway, chatting up girls around that public swimming pool became a source of something like hope. That also supplied plenty of laughs, which in those days were also scarce.

Even when it led nowhere. Which it most often did. Somehow, the act of overcoming my adolescent fear of rejection and its subsequent embarrassment left me feeling like I had done something. Though, if asked, I could not tell you even now what it might have been.

And from here, the odd time when I might think of those sunny days, I try to recall them as my earliest attempts at improving race relations.

Fortunately, a quick jump into the shocking chill of that unheated pool soon did away with the uncountable erections. Most were earned after trying to chat up one of the countless young women seated around it. And, surrounded as I was by so much female beauty while shielded with so little clothing in those days, only masturbation enabled chat of any kind.

Most times, the more vigorous a bout of onanism engaged in beforehand, the better my ability to chat with young women, often wearing the scantiest of swimwear, later.

But maybe, in the faces of those children of European refugees of the Second World War, also victims of an unseen conflict, there echoed undeniable familiarity.

For many of them had moved to Canada because of the evil of the holocaust. With others, force of arms or ruthless economic circumstance leftover from the senseless war drove them to abandon ancestral homes.

Now, like the first people of Canada, whether First Nation, Inuit, or Metis, those once called Polish, Jewish, or German, faced a stark and absolute choice. Because in this new world, the immigrants must choose between the wreckage of a long dead but treasured past or the unwelcome values of a crude and unknown society.

As we, the displaced Indigenous refugees of an unwanted confederation, must learn to fend for ourselves if we are to survive a life among its ruins.

Under the cold jets of a shower at my Aunt's Burnaby apartment that morning, the scent of the lower mainland's heavily treated water took me back to K Park. Near at once, the unknown misery of my transexual sister's young life, shrouded in the mystery of so many years of it spent out of my sight, seemed nearby.

There, on the morning before I would accompany my mother to arrange her funeral, the endless nightmare of what could only have been, revealed itself.

And even now, the useless tears torment me.

43

In those days before the rise of the smart phone and text messaging, the flip phone ruled Canada's mobile world.

To keep up profits while dodging the cost of progress, meanwhile, a telecom oligarchy born from deregulating the industry built a system of pricey 'roaming' charges.

That made the use of cell phones outside clearly defined geographic limits crazy expensive.

For decades, despite being wrapped in thousands of miles of twisted pair and fiber optic cable while living next door to the world's leading economy, Canadians would pay far more for all types of telephone and internet services than people living elsewhere on the planet.

At this writing, a near monopoly tightly controls Canada's telecom industry.

And the country sports phone and internet service costs ranked among the highest on earth.

There on the British Columbia coast, my eldest brother and I were a long way from our shared home base of Alberta. And more than a provincial border, mountain range and thirteen hundred kilometers of natural beauty stood between us. With the price of any call inflated by a varied amount-per-minute depending on time of day, cost served as a major limiting factor when staying in touch with either work or family.

The sound of a cell phone ringing when so far away from work on a family emergency was, thus, among the most unwelcome. When my big brother's flip phone rang the day before my sister

Sharon's funeral, at least it was not work. But even taking that into account, the call breaking into our chain restaurant lunch brought little good news.

Though on the bright side, keeping it short allowed big brother to limit the cost.

"So," he said, "the kid's not going to be there."

My eldest brother snapped the lid of his cellphone closed on itself.

And, much as I had been detained for losing my temper and missed my sister's wedding years before, our youngest brother would suffer the same fate now. At distant Winnipeg, where he celebrated her passing in the company of what was rumored to be too familiar whisky, grief caused the loss of his temper. In jail, he awaited remand because of turning loose aging but still lethal skills learned in the ring.

Manitoba's court system, in recess over the long weekend, would thus prevent his attending our sister's funeral.

By then, like his remaining siblings, our youngest brother was divorced. Unlike either of us, however, he was blessed with two children of his own. And sadly, his turning up in jail after a binge was no longer big news.

After speaking with the ex-wife, my eldest brother was assured our youngest was in the usual good health. Of course, younger brother also sent regrets along with condolences. The former sister-in-law also confirmed they would be at the airport when mom returned to Winnipeg after the funeral.

He reported this to me after closing the phone.

"I guess his kids will be going to school soon enough, eh?"

He asked after putting the little cell phone into a coat pocket.

I nodded. About the same time, with lingering and conflicted guilt, I then recalled not seeing my younger brother since his daughter's birth years earlier. Since his marriage, we had tried to stay away from one another, more than less.

Mostly because of his trying to stay married. And, like many in the extended family wanting also to give up the wild life, he made the best choice. In the early days of his marriage, my youngest brother wanted little more than a chance to be a husband. A tough ask for any rounder on the road to reform, I was later told he returned to school and worked hard to make a home and build a career in technology.

Though despite his desire for upward mobility, like most brown folks in Canada, widespread systemic racism suggested he stay down.

Marriage looked set to change his life for the better. And spending too much time with the randy older brother, a spend-thrift raconteur long divorced, with countless romantic failures to his credit, made little sense to either of us. He also told me it made his wife nervous when I hung around. In my mind, staying away from them was being polite. So, maybe to honor how close we once had been despite the increasing divergence of our adult lives, we tried for a long-distance phone call once a year.

Most times, we also caught up a little whenever the scattered remnants of the family got together for holiday meals. There, between screenings of the same old movies on TV, we might manage a semi-private three-minute chat when doing chores, meeting by the garbage cans or over the sink, as we long ago had to as foster children.

For a few years, to self-absorbed me, it seemed those snatches of catch-up talk would be enough to maintain the fraying rope of family tying us together.

To further add to his lofty status as baby of the family, he cemented a place as mom's surviving favorite by being first to give her grandchildren. And since their much-heralded arrival within a few years of each other, my youngest brother's children proved to be the greatest source of both pride and joy in her world.

Again, my thoughts turned to our mom. Once more, I wondered at her tenuous grip on the ugly reality of this world in which we all must live.

44

As usual, an out-of-control ego proved the source of concern. Because my mom, despite her son's unfounded fears, spent the time focused on seeing to her late daughter's last wishes. While caring for the needs of the living. I recall being pleased by the few points of dissent between the people helping our family. In contrast to when my father passed some years before, my sister's funeral would prove a relaxed affair.

And the source of few quarrels.

Old friends and surprising numbers of the extended family, escaped to the warm west coast after tiring of the brutal snow and dangerous ice of winter on the prairies, hosted a post funeral gathering common to earlier life on the reserve. And like it often is at funerals, I recall the food served there being as weirdly close to spectacular as amateur cooks can make it. Because most times, and I have no idea why, honoring the dead seems to bring the inner catering chef out of poor folks.

To my undying shame, it turns out I am one of those freaks who rates a funeral based on the quality of the food served after it.

Also, I will admit to being caught short by the turn of events. To his credit, my gracious eldest brother gave the money needed for what is an increasingly expensive process. He also told me he was more than happy to do it, though he was likely trying to make me feel better about my latest cash flow problem. Anyway, most times, the actual cost of such an event is measured in something other than money.

When it came time to bury my dad, that sure seemed to be the case.

As his oldest surviving child, my grieving mother asked me to function as executor of my intestate father's legal affairs. I was proud to be asked and devoted myself to the task, despite a misery as deep as any I have known. To this day, the blur of memory is all that restrains my disgust at the petty disputes resulting from trying to deliver a funeral service that comforted the living while respecting the atheist values of my late father. Stuck between the supernatural belief of those who loved him longest and the scientific facts preferred by the man, it seemed I managed only to anger most people.

His surviving friends, with their families creating a traffic jam near two miles long between the small town's church and the rural cemetery, were angered by too few military accolades.

The church service outraged the younger brother.

While dispensing with the estate disgusted my elder brother.

My sister, happily, after asking how I was doing, told me she could not have cared less about any of it.

And the pallbearers chosen, along with my decision to take over his ranch, outraged the extended family.

I seem to recall a girlfriend of the time expressing what seemed sincere enough surprise at the placid response with which I greeted the remarks impugning my character. And, maybe fortunately, I was in too much pain to care about reacting to any of it.

Besides that, like others before her in a short-term position, she was long ago assigned to the scrapheap of memory.

Anyway, the food served at the gathering held in the town hall at Hodgson after my dad's contentious funeral was delicious. Much as the respect the community held for one of its last surviving local war heroes was clear in the condolences shared by hundreds of mourners. Many of whom were children and grandchildren of long dead comrades-in-arms. To a plate, the ladies of his remote home town showed their love for my father on that day, and I will go to my grave most grateful for it.

And it bears repeating, if only to honor an unseemly obsession.

The food served at my sister Sharon's funeral was great.

45

Tall trees overlooked family and friends spread around an open gravesite in the rare sunshine of a rapidly warming lower mainland summer morning. A churchman, his stripe unknown to me but included with the funeral package bought from the Hastings Street parlor, stood at one end of a hole that gaped from wet earth beneath a polished wood coffin. He awaited the mourners with ebbing patience, uncomfortable in a dark suit and trapped by rising heat.

As he again cleared his throat, family gathered around the final resting place, suspended above the grave by red canvas straps of a mechanized lift.

In a few brief minutes, the more than less usual speech was complete.

Once you have been to a few, funerals play out much alike and my sister Sharon's would be little different. Many people aside from myself cried. And much comfort was taken by a public display of grief at the loss of another ever-unknown soldier from within our midst. The collective bosom, in this case taking the physical shape of local relatives and friends, emitted a communal sigh of mourning.

It must suffice to calm the fears of the many soldiers left behind.

Who knows if there is any more to it than that? Not me, and that is for sure. All I know is what I have had to live through, and it does not amount to much. But the thing is, and no offense to the academics for whom I hold undying respect, most times life does not go according to what has been written about it.

And while easy enough to write something down that way, grief only presents itself with clearly defined stages in a textbook. In corporeal reality, the place where most of us spend what we think of as time, feelings and other such nonsense things come and go as they please.

Often, they are unmindful of words in books, plans well or otherwise made and the unlimited demands of daily living. Just as, for many of us, there can be things with which we do not ever come to grips in a way satisfactory to the imagination.

It must also be said, despite our species-wide claims otherwise, that experience of what we call reality, mostly, happens there.

And perhaps because of it, the pain and mystery of death has forced us to come up with all kinds of coping mechanisms. For many of us, however, managing grief and loss must become a way of life.

Anyway, by now I have long ago decided practice is the only thing that allows any of us to survive it.

And, happily for the rest of the family, life had by then given my mother plenty of chances to learn how to ride out the misery. Though I am sure she would have left without further training if given a choice. But all the same, as she entered the later stages of what proved a long life, it seemed she could channel mind-numbing agony into service to others. I know that for me, stumbling around at Sharon's funeral like a cross between a new-foaled colt and a bawling two-year-old child, my mom's resolute strength pulled me through it.

I do not remember being embarrassed. Grief does that to me. Or maybe it shows there is a little good in even the worst things the universe can dream up to throw at a person. After all, until going to the first funeral I can remember, I was too concerned with what others might think of me to be caught shedding a tear in public.

The burial of my brothers had changed that.

The unknown relief, felt after sharing tears with family and friends, also shone light on a part of life about which I had been ignorant. But I did not know that when I bawled like a sick calf way back when. And I would certainly have traded anything those tears might be worth to bring my brothers back among the living.

I can say that now, when it can no longer do me any harm and it is too late to do any good. But then, like everyone else in the family, all I could do was cry. Nor do I know why, standing there, in warm shade thrown by the overgrown trees of that semi-tropical urban wasteland, those thoughts flooded my aching head.

Because, just like that, our much beloved sister Sharon was also gone.

46

"All right," he said, "I'm going to tell you something."

Under the high sun of a late September afternoon in central Manitoba, we stood next to one another on the porch step of his remote cabin. With a job awaiting my return to the faraway city, I was in something of a hurry to leave the distant ranch that had once been my home. Through a work week just passed, he visited both my mom and his doctor at Winnipeg. And I had undertaken the six-hour round-trip needed to drive my father to his rural home on Sunday afternoon.

In his mid-sixties, my dad was by then a diminished version of the man I knew as a child. As he entered a third decade of life after one of North America's early open-heart surgeries, he struggled with other health issues. Serious, and common to Indigenous people, he also dealt with high blood pressure.

The powerful rancher of my youth, able to deal with anything or anyone that might prove bold enough to challenge him, now lived only in memory.

"If it wasn't for the damned pills," he said, "I'd have been dead years ago."

We sat next to one another in the cab of my decade-old pickup truck. Only a moment earlier, he appeared to suffer a heart attack. As the blood drained from his face, he struggled to withdraw a pill from the bottle pulled out of a shirt pocket. He popped a tiny white button under his tongue and then slowly returned to what I recognized as normal.

"What happened?"

I asked a few minutes later when he appeared to have recovered well enough to speak.

"I believe they call it a mild heart attack," he said.

As usual, his voice was matter of fact.

"You're not kidding," I said, "are you, dad?"

As I watched, he shook his head.

"No," he said, "but I sometimes wish I was."

More than a little stunned, I made no reply.

"Come on," he said, "when a man waits months for an appointment to see some high-tone sonofabitch, he better not be late for it, eh?"

The clinic was on an upper floor. As we stood in the lobby waiting for an elevator, I felt his elbow nudge my ribs. An attractive older woman in the company of what looked like her daughter had appeared next to us. Ever the charmer, he raised an eyebrow and gave a tilt of his still handsome face, indicating the prurient desire.

I shook my head, stifled a laugh, and grinned back at him. Despite suffering a heart attack only a few moments earlier, there he stood, ready with an extra-marital hard-on. And so long as I have a memory, that is the one I will keep of my dad. To the end, not one thought of surrender, not so long as there was a pretty woman left alive on his earth.

Maybe because I left his home under a cloud of misunderstanding or because of us both growing older, my dad and I eventually came to know one another as well as seemed right for a father and son. At least, to me, it seemed that way. Anyway, as I did not ask him about it while he was here, I guess we will never know what he might have thought about it.

But plainly, I felt myself close enough to my dad.

Raised themselves by a generation that believed kids should be seen but not heard, everything I knew about parenting came from the example he and my mom gave. Unfortunately, because of the various mental and emotional fractures suffered by our parents before and after our births, myself and most of my siblings would endure a good portion of our childhoods as foster children. The force of the reality our parents would deal with in their lives, however, lies beyond my ability to fairly grasp from here. So, to say we missed out on the best of what they might have had to offer us because of it, would likely be an understatement.

Anyway, to my grave, I will believe they gave us the best of what remained.

"What's up, pops?"

I remember smiling at him that day, again surprised by how much even I could see the physical resemblance between us. For love or money, there would be no denying I was near close enough to be considered his doppelganger.

By that time, I was also quite proud of it and remain so to this day. And again, as it made no sense to ask him, I cannot tell you what he might have thought about it. Because, while he enjoyed a bullshit story as much as anyone I have yet known, he was not a man to give any kind of instruction.

Likewise, he would offer advice only rarely and most times under protest.

"You were born with two eyes and two ears," he said, "but only one mouth. And, if I have to tell you again, I'm going to whip your ass, boy. You got it?"

I nodded.

"What do you say?"

The eyes staring at five-year-old me seemed to bore into my chest, passing cold judgement on my thudding heart.

"Yes, sir?"

My dad grinned.

"That's right," he said, "now come on, let's get you boys some grub, eh?"

We had arrived moments before in the company of an uncle. Another breakdown and hospital for our tortured mother in the city meant the two youngest would spend at least a summer with their bachelor father.

And even though I would not ever see even one of the many demons tormenting my dad in a physical form, as a boy, I recall knowing they were always nearby.

"If I know it's coming," he said, "and I'm pretty sure now I will, I'm going to saddle my black horse and take a last ride."

He paused a moment, but only long enough to silence me with a glance.

"When the time comes," my dad said, "you send them out to the west ridge overlooking the pond where we used to watch the beavers play when you and your brother were little pissers. I'll be there, watching myself a last sunset."

A lump rose in my throat and a fear unlike any I had known filled my chest.

"Don't talk like that, dad," I said, "you're going to outlive all of us."

He waved an enormous and still heavily callused hand.

"That'll do." he said, "You hold up your end. Just as you've been taught."

Though close to tears, I could only nod. And when the terrible day arrived, with certain pride filling what remained of my broken heart, I did as he had taught me.

47

In those days, from a rundown two-story Victorian Revival on Furby Street between Sergeant and Ellice Avenue, with a couple of fellow desperadoes I ran an illegal after-hours drinking joint then known as a 'booze can' on weekend nights.

The windows were boarded over from inside and girls worked from two of four bedrooms upstairs. And the joint augmented my seasonal contracting business income while giving rent-free housing to a couple of the partners.

Five hundred per week, paid in cash on Monday nights, kept us safe from both cops and the wars of consolidation then unfolding on Canada's streets from coast to coast.

On weekend nights, members of a local club parked their bikes at street and alley entrances to the house. While a squad car rolled past on the half hour. Anyone foolish enough to think about raising a ruckus either on the street or inside the latter-day speakeasy was soon calmed. Those not impressed enough to quiet down were left to the mercy of the fierce professionals in charge of keeping that joint from disturbing the neighbors.

I recall thinking it good business for all concerned.

Few people not frequenting the place knew the address, and even less that I lived there. As despite a residential lease, the house was rented for the business, and I made a point of not having guests there outside of operating hours.

So, to hear an early morning knock at the front door, on a weekday, was plenty more than surprising.

I left a working girl sleeping in my king size waterbed and threw on a pair of gym shorts before stumbling down the rickety stairs. The pounding continued and seemed to grow more ominous the closer I came to the door.

"I'm coming!"

Still barely awake, what emerged was less than a shout, but more than room level. The incessant knocking continued. Whomever waited on the other side of the security door must not have heard me.

"Hang on!"

Even I heard the frustration in my voice that time. After unlocking a trio of guardians holding back the dawn, I flung the heavy steel-reinforced inner door open. Only a flimsy screen stood between me and the covered porch.

There, with tears streaming down both cheeks, stood my mother.

"It's your dad," she said, "they can't find him."

I recall a feeling like my body deflating as I stood there.

Perhaps a few seconds later, my dad's patient and lifelong training of his eldest surviving child kicked in, and I opened the door to embrace my mom. After what seemed forever, we moved into the living room of the grotesquery in which I then resided. We sat on one of several nearby faux leather sofas.

In only a few moments, while comforting my mom, I got the news about my dad.

My uncle, a customer and thus aware of where I could be found in the event of emergency, had driven her to the place. He joined us on the sofa. Her younger brother was well known for devotion to his older sisters. The fellow was also a lifelong friend of my father, and plainly struggled to hold himself together.

And despite the den of inequity surrounding us, we began mourning the loss of a great man and forever unknown soldier there.

I do not know how long we wailed in that room, but later, I recall being grateful to the young woman waiting upstairs when she did not interrupt. And though I cannot say for sure, it is likely she received a nice tip on the way out the door.

Anyway, there in that filthy shithouse, the three of us cried for a while.

Not too much later, after my mom and her brother left for home, I called the Mounties at Fisher Branch. And told them where to find my dad. Before soon leaving the city. I traveled alone and pointed my pickup truck towards Highway Seventeen and the morgue at distant Hodgson's Percy E. Moore hospital. There, by the time I pulled into the parking lot hours later, my father's earthly remains awaited identification.

Before tending to the business, I spoke with the Sergeant who located my dad and brought his body to the hospital.

As he told me he would, my dad removed both bridle and saddle from his black horse when he arrived at the ridge on the west quarter of his property. There, together with him, me and my youngest brother had long ago spent many an evening. As, hidden among the trees of a rocky outcropping which overlooked a pond, we had watched while an extended family of beavers worked to improve their home.

His dog Lundy went with him on the last ride. Along with his favorite black horse, she stood guard as my father enjoyed a final sunset over the land to whose patient care he long ago devoted his life.

And there, in the company of dear friends who loved him unconditionally, my father left this earth.

I recall thanking the hated Mountie for his trouble, and despite my lifelong rancor at site of the uniform, meaning it. A few moments later, in the cool of what passed for the small-town hospital's morgue, to satisfy my duty to him and for their records, I confirmed the man brought in was my father.

There are many things for which I am now and will ever be grateful, but none will surpass the gift granted to me on that long-ago day. For even now, carefully gilded by existential misery and survivor's guilt, the memory remains. And so, for all my time, I will be grateful to fate and circumstance for allowing me to experience it.

As there, on a cold steel slab beneath the pale glow of fluorescent tubes overhead, my father lay in wait for a son's last verification of his identity. And when I stood only feet away from the sheet-covered gurney on which he lay, the young physician hung his head while keeping silent. I remember taking a deep breath and stepping to my dad's side as the unknown doctor moved to lift a pale sheet.

To reveal the handsome face waiting, as ever patient, beneath it.

There to greet me when the sheet was pulled back lay my beloved father. Forever wearing the warm and gentle smile remembered well by all those blessed with the good fortune to know him.

48

The pomegranate is a fruit grown since ancient times in the Mideast. And brought to North America by the endless onslaught of globalization begun in the long-forgotten past. Since, the fruit is grown as a cash crop in once desertified areas of the lower forty-eight of the United States. And became a widely stocked item at Canada's grocery stores by the late nineteen-seventies.

I did not then know that history. Seated in the neat kitchen of our small apartment, I watched as my mom worked with caution over a well-scarred wood cutting board. She hovered there, handling what looked to be a red piece of round fruit, a little bigger than a baseball. In her expert hand, she casually wielded a paring knife as sharp as any shaving razor's blade.

She first took a narrow slice from one end of the red ball, creating a flat spot. After that, placing the thing onto the board with its cut end down, she repeatedly split the red skin from near a barely pointed but unmarked top to its sliced bottom.

Next, taking the cutting board holding the red ball with her, she moved a few steps to work at the sink.

Into a large bowl first placed in the sink and filled with cold water, she dunked the fruit. A moment later, I stood to watch as her dexterous but careful fingers opened the red baseball, much like spreading the petals of a flower, by sliding along the lengthwise cuts made in its skin.

When she did, exposed beneath the water were countless examples of what looked like miniature berries, each a brilliant scarlet.

And plainly, awaiting hunger's discovery.

Under the gentle coaxing of her fingertips, the delicate and near translucent fruits, along with a portion of white and inedible pith, were removed from the safety of the plant's innards. The delicate red balls collected on the bottom of the bowl.

While the pale and useless pith floated to the surface, awaiting disposal in the garbage can beneath the sink.

I stood silent and watched. Not only amazed by the weird fruit but also quite stoned on the newly arrived Panama Red shared by a classmate after school.

Along with older sister Sharon, my mom lived at the run-down apartment with me. She was by then long separated from my dad. After tracking her to a Calgary booze can, I hitchhiked out there and invited her to join me back at Winnipeg. I told her of a desire to leave my trades job and return to finish high school in the city. And pressed her to support the plan. In no uncertain terms, she was a mess when I found her at the dangerous joint sunlight revealed to the surrounding foothills.

By then, back at Winnipeg, sister Sharon was running a string of working girls full-time. With a solid if small-time thing peddling mostly nickel and dime bags of weed going myself, money was not the problem causing either of us grief.

Big sister had no legal guardianship of her younger brother, and my return to high school needed the signature of a local parent.

Sadly, just then we seemed to be fresh out.

At the time, it was clear that addictions were in control of my mom. While it proved simple enough to convince her to return with me to Winnipeg, keeping her together to sign even the few simple forms needed to register me for school turned out to be quite a job. And despite a concerted best effort, within only weeks it seemed keeping her from committing suicide might also prove too much for me and my sister.

The years after my return to high school would involve more time shuttling mom back and forth to the psych ward than spent in classrooms.

More than once, lost in a drug and alcohol induced panic and believing herself under attack from someone or something known only to a tortured mind, she attacked me. Often with weapons, including knives, when I came home from school. After wrestling the danger away from her, if not calmed with more liquor or soon knocked out by the drugs she had already taken, many times her out-of-control psychosis required an ambulance.

As, until the religious awakening at the Christian church downtown, our cherished mom appeared well on the way to long-term or even permanent commitment.

Her sudden recovery was at first hard to believe. But as years passed, and she emerged as herself despite the earlier struggles, it would also prove impossible to deny. Anyway, most of that came later.

In the early days, with no pun intended, our shared apartment became known as a high-traffic spot.

With mom trying to get started in recovery, my sister secretly running a string of hookers and me dealing weed. All from a basement one-bedroom where St. John's Avenue met Main Street in Winnipeg's north end.

It seemed there was always something happening. Mostly because of how my sister and I earned our livings, there were people coming and going no matter the time of night or day. But, as society does its best to ignore poor folks everywhere, our Canadian neighbors we happy to leave us to our own devices so long as we paid the rent on time.

Due mainly to the hustling of my sister and myself, we did that while allowing our mom time to recover.

After removing the last of the scarlet berries from it, my mom strained them into another large bowl. It seemed there must be hundreds of them. I learned, sometime later, they were seeds, and not what my eyes presumed them to be.

"Come on," she said, "I want you to try these."

I nodded, more than ready to do as I was told.

She placed the bowl onto the kitchen table between us. A moment later, she handed me a tablespoon, along with a dish towel.

"They're really juicy," she said, "and the juice stains anything it touches, so be careful not to get any on your clothes."

I nodded again.

"How do I eat them?"

She grinned across the table at me, plainly enjoying the moment and, as usual, pleased to show me something new.

"Like eating a berry," she said, "but a delicate one."

She picked up the spoon next to her in one hand and, with a towel in the other, scooped up several of the plump red seeds. And holding the cloth under her spoon to catch any spills, she popped the lot of them into her mouth. Upon seeing her eyes light up with delight, seconds later I followed her example.

And for sure, the fruit has been cultivated since ancient times due to a unique and delectable flavor. Despite countless supernatural claims made to otherwise support its ongoing popularity among our kind. Anyway, in less than a moment, they transported me to a place of warm comfort.

It was my first taste of that fruit of an unknown and distant foreign land. My mother smiled as she watched me eat it. Nowadays, I like to think she believed it would be the first of many new things I would try.

But I said nothing then, instead grinning as I again dug my spoon into the bowl on the table between us. She laughed at me, and it sounded much like that of the many teenaged Caucasian girls at school on those days I chose to attend.

"I'm glad you like them my boy," she said, "they're one of few things actually good for you that are also delicious."

I recall biting into another mouthful of the red seeds, and their juice dripping like sweet blood from my lips. Even in that moment, when I would certainly have been too stoned to drive, it seemed a memory of her worth keeping.

And for it, I am grateful.

49

Along with my eldest brother, I arrived at my late sister's Burnaby apartment in the middle of a grey morning to clean the place. Not a job for the faint of heart, due to what we had learned about Sharon's last days, the brothers decided to perform a first cleaning of her home before allowing my mom and the aunts to finish it.

I have since been grateful for that as well.

By then, mom had been out of the wild life for over twenty years, and it seemed a poor time to remind her of its terms. I cannot say for sure, but it seemed to me at the time that Sharon would be grateful for the brother's doing her such a last favor. Anyway, if the places were reversed, it should certainly be important to me.

So, despite my fears, I was more than willing to do it.

But when we pulled into the parking lot of the apartment complex with only drizzling rain to greet us, I will admit to almost losing my nerve. As the rented car's engine came to a stop and the reality of what we must do next settled onto me, I was forced to take a deep breath to steady unsure nerves. For a moment, my breakfast, tasty enough when eaten a half hour earlier, was no longer sitting as it once had.

"Well?"

His voice sounded at least as hesitant as I felt.

"Yah," I said, "let's get after it, eh?"

I remember wanting to sound committed to our task.

Their former home at first seemed much like the apartment where I had earlier seen them living together. It was neat and decorated according to Sharon's bohemian tastes. A closer look revealed the signs of decline we wanted to remove from the place. Before letting mom and the aunts catalog possessions and clean our late sister's home a final time. While the decades of our adult lives were spent half a nation apart, I was sure my sister's stash would not be hard for me to find.

And aside from the unreasonable fact of them not being there, the home of a deceased person changes not one bit when they leave this earth.

But the mere act of walking into a place either inhabited by the dead or not your own, if not breaking and entering, creates a feeling that memory will label disquiet. And, while a known source of discomfort for many people, the effect is further amped up if said home belongs to a family member.

In a bid to break the grip of coming morbidity, I soon found and switched on the stereo in the living room.

Then, after sending my eldest brother to check what I knew should be an empty medicine cabinet in the bathroom, I removed a plastic-wrapped stash of smack from the fridge's freezer. As he next searched through barren drawers in the living room buffet, I grabbed a sealed bag of weed from Sharon's bedside table. I said nothing to him about the dope, instead stashing the bags in my socks for safe keeping.

And mostly because I was unsure of the safety of the smack, I flushed it a few minutes later while stepping into the bathroom for a piss. The weed, however, which I knew would be a powerful Indica best used as a sleep aid, came home with me. As usual in matters of taste, my big sister's choice of herb would later prove excellent.

But, with empty liquor bottles, used needles and burnt spoons littering the apartment, only after donning gloves could we safely remove the assortment of junkie crap. And though I am not sure how many tears we brothers cried through those few hours spent taking out the detritus of addiction, there were many.

But when done, we had cleaned her place of any sign of the addict's tools. While sister Sharon's home could yet be called a mess, what remained to greet my mom and her sisters was as innocent as we could make it.

It was only when pulling out of the parking lot, seated next to each other in the rented sedan with eyes still reddened, that it occurred to me. Through the hours spent in the place, despite the countless tears shed and many shared hugs of comfort, we had not spoken so much as a single word.

And just then, driving to the home of an aunt to deliver the keys to Sharon's empty apartment to our grieving mother, there seemed no need for talk.

50

A few years earlier, my experience had been different.

For much like the man himself, his place was remote and impassive when viewed from a distance and dark and inscrutable if seen from up close. As I had by then found out, living alone means a different set of rules. While choosing isolation also meant circumstances unimagined to those enjoying the modern comforts available in the civilized world.

To me, it seemed my dad chose what most pleased him.

In that place, he enjoyed neither electricity nor plumbing. For heat through the bitter cold of Manitoba's lengthy winters, he burned wood cut by his own hand.

Anyway, the young lady holding my hand had departed soon after spending the weekend of his funeral at the empty cabin with me. Maybe due to everything else going on then, or perhaps not, what we might have one day would prove a casualty of that time. And when looking back, I cannot say if it was for better or worse.

Because once I got there, it took me a couple of years to leave.

And in case I did not say it earlier, I have never been sure if sleep is routine practice for being dead or if death is little more than a permanent nap. To me, each seems located within the elastic boundary of reason. Though I will also admit not having a firm grasp on the scientific implications of either circumstance proving a fact. Anyway, so far, no amount of published research documenting brain activity in people sleeping has dislodged the stubborn mystery of either nightly or permanent event.

To this point, I remain near as willing to be convinced of one as the other.

On most nights, the dreams seemed as real as the life I was leading. In them, I was most often a child and frightened. Then, from nowhere, he would appear and fear at once vanished. Many times, in the dreams we hunted together much as we had in life and spoke of things I later could not remember.

Which did not surprise me upon waking, as I recall he spoke little to any of the children in our home.

But as in reality, it made little difference to how I or anyone else would feel about him. Because even in dreams, my dad seemed to be made of stuff more solid than a world constantly rearranging itself around him.

And maybe after a while, I might have preferred to sleep and dream of him more than dealing with the demands made by his death. Nowadays, I also wonder if that might be what the physicists call a wormhole.

Though, like I said before, uncertainty seems to make all the difference.

Unknown to me, as executor of his estate, a thorough review and report on the personal affects, assets and liabilities of the intestate deceased was required. And like it or not, I would have to review my father's personal life and business holdings.

In keeping with the routine privacy of his lifestyle, my dad's filing system on behalf of each proved unique and mysterious as its creator. I got help from his lawyer.

The fellow enjoyed a drink too much for my comfort. He also practiced from the mess of an office at the far-off town of Ashern, Manitoba. Together, we completed and filed the estate's legal paperwork.

It took only a single calendar year from the day of my father's demise.

There were kitchen drawers overfilled with paper. And from between the pages of notebooks hidden under his mattress, what appeared an endless supply of personal notes and business filings seemed to bloom. Alone at the distant ranch, I reviewed every handwritten scrap of paper I could find or track down by request of the often-half-drunk lawyer.

With the community still living by terms of a party-line telephone system, I am sure most folks were aware of what was happening. And while they would offer sympathy when I made it into town, they left me to my own devices out there until we settled the estate. Likewise, among the clan, there seemed great reticence to interfere with the legal process, despite the lengthy wait for it to run a usual course.

As with funeral arrangements, I ignored any wants of my own as I followed my mom's orders when disposing of my father's estate.

Afterwards, spread out across the country as we again were, little room for complaint remained without starting a pointless war encouraged only by lawyers. And make no mistake, the poor folks I have known, no matter the color of their skin, are as messed up about money as everyone else.

Ever a humble man, my father passed leaving few debts for me to settle on his behalf.

A chequing account at the Fisher Branch credit union contained funds enough to clear them. The land on which he also worked was owned outright. The cabin in which he lived, built by his own hands though not to code and of little resale value according to a realtor hired to evaluate the property, was also free and clear. His equine stock, free of mortgage and amounting to several dozen mares rented to a regional PMU farm, produced income enough to pay the property's annual taxes. The half section of cleared but clay-bottomed soil surrounding the cabin, assigned an optimistic value of one hundred dollars per acre, despite its remote locale, also belonged only to him.

When my thorough search revealed not so much as a single whisky bottle, it was also clear my dad had died sober.

And for reasons unknown, that continues to please me as much as anything I have ever learned about him.

51

Her name was Veronica, but everyone called her Vickie.

When introduced to me, she was a voluptuous twenty-one. Like a ripened flower, she seemed about to burst from the clothes she barely wore. By then, even my eldest brother considered her a ravishing beauty.

I, however, was sixteen.

Shortly after meeting her, a mix of teenage hormones and unbridled imagination produced, for me, a kind of personal hell not previously known. And if I am telling it straight, maybe it shames me to recall how often I relieved myself in the shower to a dream of her beauty.

As not so long after meeting, we grew to be, supposedly, great pals. Because at the time, five years might as well have been a century.

She moved into the apartment of her older sister on a floor above us. Her sister was also a friend of my mom. A day or a few after she moved in, the sisters joined my mother at our apartment for a catch up over coffee. It was a humid afternoon in late June, as I recall, and I interrupted the soiree by coming home early after classes at St. John's High.

Elder sister Kaye introduced me to Veronica, a petite beauty with a perfect tan. She then stood up from the kitchen table to shake my hand.

In the fashion of those times, she wore a white tank top over full and braless breasts. Faded blue denim shorts cut high in the hip revealed firm muscled thighs, tanned dark above chiseled calves and white running shoes. Lustrous and thick, chestnut hair streaked with natural highlights hung loose past her shoulders. While white teeth gleamed from between red painted lips with the hint of a natural pout. Her blue eyes were evenly spaced, and piercing, above a pixie's saucily upturned nose. They seemed to stare, both cool and frank, into the blind desire at once alight in my juvenile heart.

"Pleased to meet you," she said.

A smile of penetrating beauty flashed, defiant in response to my naked lust.

"Um, ya," I said, "likewise."

My reply, stolen from an old movie, emerged with a stumble.

And despite the hint of a stammer, I remember doing my best to play it cool. Until maybe fifteen seconds later, when I had to leave the room.

The jeans I wore, with widely flared legs of a disco style only just arrived in the remote north, were both tight and revealing. It would be weeks before I could be around her without getting a near instant erection. That was not only obvious but also distracting enough to prevent further talk.

So long as she lived with her sister upstairs, I would spend much of my time at home as the proverbial hungry dog staring up at a butcher's shop window.

But even at sixteen, I had already spent enough time with the working girls to know Vickie wanted only friendship. She was not there because of either desire or accident. Violent domestic abuse, as usual ignored by the so-called Canadian justice system, forced her to move there. Older sister Kaye, now a divorced victim of the same treatment, could give only tenuous sanctuary.

Anyway, over that summer Vickie and I shared a friendship. Easily as frustrating as it was instructive for me, the mooning lasted only until she departed for a new life on the distant west coast.

Her big sister, Kaye, helped with Sharon's funeral arrangements.

When we reacquainted at the cemetery, more than half a continent and twenty years stood between me and the girls. But as divorced and single Vickie pressed her body against mine, the hug we exchanged lingered a moment too long. And in the smile shared as we drew apart, I knew at once a teen boy's fantasy would soon be replaced by the carnal certainty of manhood.

Later, when greeting mourners at the repast held at Kaye's spotless Surrey home with my big brother, thoughts of Vickie distracted me. The warm sun beamed. And despite making funeral talk with relatives in the backyard, I recall it being a struggle to ignore the insistent throb of nature's call.

As despite the misery of Sharon's passing and many shared tears at a well-attended funeral, thoughts of what lay ahead consumed me. Through passage of that long day, I recall my attention focusing more on a knee-length black dress than grief. That adorned the yet fit and well-maintained physique of onetime gal pal Vickie.

To that point, in relative terms, for each of us the years had been kind.

And for her, instead of impediment, the five-year age difference now made the coming event something of a conquest. I am also pretty sure everyone at the funeral was aware of the flirtation between us. But as usual, I proved willing to overlook a few raised eyebrows if it meant getting what I wanted.

We met at her North Vancouver apartment. A few hours later, as she slept next to me, I stole from between cool satin sheets now stained with bodily fluids and commingled sweat. Not even thoughts of a morning repeat of what turned out a better than hoped for version of the unlived past would convince me to stay.

Less than an hour later, I let myself into a New Westminster apartment with the paranoid stealth of a break and enter artist.

The place was, of course, middle of the night still. On a sofa in the living room, covered with blankets but not snoring, lay the familiar shape of my eldest brother. Across the room from him, our kind aunt had prepared a makeshift bed on the floor for me. After stopping into the bathroom for a piss, I stripped to briefs and rolled into the sleeping bag laid atop a quilt.

"You ok, my bud?"

With our mom and her sisters asleep in bedrooms down the hall, he spoke in a voice barely above a whisper. I responded in kind.

"It's all good," I said, "sorry to disturb you."

I remember him grunting.

"Hope she was after all these years," he said.

In the darkness, I heard him chuckle.

"Like fine wine, bro," I said, "better for the age."

From the sofa across the room, came a snort of barely controlled laughter.

And falling into sleep on the carpeted floor, I recall a grin of certain knowledge that seemed unwilling to leave my face.

52

I have wondered often since about memory. Between hands mostly, when action slows at the weekly private game or if waiting for a casino table seat. But no amount of it has so far eased my ongoing existential discontent.

Not that I am a scholar, so do not get the wrong idea.

After all, it is likely most people waiting on cards to fall have plenty of thoughts pass them by. So, following suit does not make me special.

Besides that, from here, it looks as much like history as anything else. But then again, most times I find so little difference between philosophy and nonsense it is near impossible to tell them apart. And so, perhaps at its end my story gives little balm for what might have ailed either reader or writer.

Sadly, for most of us, it seems life often turns out that way.

Anyway, as they will, our family soon dispersed after the latest funeral. Like now forever missing sister Sharon, both immediate and extended clan seemed to dissipate, much as fog in the light of dawn after a night of rain. By the next evening's fall, they were all beyond reach of any campfire's light.

And for those carrying on, postmodern life's routines would then demand the attention once reserved for either grief or healing.

Not only that, but around here even a single week away from the hustle ratchets up the earning pressure causing the better part of a poor man's concern. As a result, along with most of the clan, me and big brother wasted little time before pulling a Hannibal, crossing the mountains, and getting back to work.

If, however, after reading this story there lingers a notion of discontent within you, know that nothing close to it lies with me.

Because here, despite watching as the sands of time are arranged into a history more acceptable to the narrative under construction, linger instead these pictures. Of our survival. And with the facts of that story at last collected, at least so long as we communicate using language and imagination, no later revision can ever change it.

As likewise, I cannot imagine the future value of such remembrance.

So, for not only myself, but all those refugees of confederation who have gone before and each of them damned to follow, it will have to do.

Because such is the stuff of dreams. As only from the murky depths of fickle memory do stories of a past shared by unknown forebears emerge. For with history's facts soon lost and group fancy either wildly inflated or heartily denied, any culture's drift into fantasy and faith is a near certain result.

It seems plain enough, at least to me, that memory lies at the heart of an ongoing dispute between what we claim to believe versus how we continue to act.

Likewise, what is widely taught as history is most often later revealed as little more than gilded myth. In most cases, devised as part of a scheme to continue sharing wealth and privilege among the few.

For despite widely promoted fear of solo oppression by a horded many, concentrating wealth and power in an extremely limited minority has ever been the bane of collective existence.

And remains so at this writing.

Over time, and with certainty, lies repeatedly told have been widely accepted as facts.

Thus, the many barriers between us are entrenched. Our schools, thoughts, and history, forever in conflict, can only fortify the many divisions. While our world, built on foundations of inequity, ensures there can be no common historic ground between us.

Aside from empty celebrating of events that further enrich the few while forever enslaving the many.

And for all of us awaits a lifetime spent unknowing. Alert but ignorant in our distractions. Or locked in relentless toil at the same heartless grindstone from cradle to grave. Where from among a chaff of lies mixed with the ruthless facts known only by long dead kin, comes the feed upon which future inequity relies for sustenance.

How else to break such heartless chains?

Woven into the fabric of time, they exist today as part of it. To even try to separate myth from fact, meanwhile, has become absurd. As by now, seeking the illusion of freedom can appear a solo act of certain madness.

So, maybe because of all that, or everything else, I cannot say for sure if this job chose me or if I picked it. Today, it seems always to have been there, waiting patient in the forgotten dark of an unknown corner, for me to pick up the tools. And since taking them as my own, I have done my best to honor this work.

Though solitary, I was not alone. Save when needing to be. To best preserve a vision. Or when working on the task of preservation. Of this covenant, unknown but surely and forever linking these people from the hidden past with those of an untold future.

So the acts of their history, shared, may shed light on your tomorrows.

I should also point out that I do not remember wanting to share it. Not only that, but after looking it over, I am not sure there was ever a choice.

Because there is also plenty of nonsense a man will sooner recall. Much of it pleasant enough too, like 'petting in dew covered grass on teenaged summer evenings at Winnipeg'. And that, along with countless sweet nothings of similar value, is best filed under 'pretty girl with a name I can no longer remember and slender body I will not forget'.

Put it right next to stuff like 'making love parked outside a rural cemetery' or 'singing to the car radio together on the way home'. While we are at it, let us not forget 'smoking pot alone at the ranch after dad passed' and 'guilt after beating up a weaker schoolboy'.

Such horseshit is best consigned to the scrapheap of a forgotten past.

Or sitting around thinking about all the stuff I could have done to make things better but would not. Because I was too proud, or angry, or stubborn. Knowing it would have been different if I had told my side of the story. And that later, things could not ever be changed.

Time spent that way is wasted.

Every second of it.

Anyway, nowadays just about everyone should know how fickle memory is. With any luck, maybe that will be enough to get me off the hook for any perceived slights cropping up among the family.

And if not?

Well, I have always considered it best to joke with people when they will not take that other thing.

Anyway, like I said before, it will have to do.

Because there is more than catharsis within these pages. Though I will not guess what anyone else might want to say about it. I am also sure that I do not care.

But if, after reading all this, I have yet to make clear one thing, well here it is.

We are them, and they are us. As you, most certainly, are me. And all the dreams that live in your imagination, at any time and in whatever place, be they good, bad, or indifferent, are ever possible. For not one thing is, nor can be, just as it seems. All that, and plenty more, is what this history of our people teaches.

The way it was. Not what the winners said about it.

And maybe most of all, for that I am grateful.

END

T.F. Pruden

Thorsby, Alberta, Canada

August 25, 2021

ABOUT THE AUTHOR

T.F. Pruden is a novelist born in Canada. He spent much of his life learning to write fiction while touring the North American hinterland performing music under a stage name. After retiring from life on the road he began writing and publishing a series of literary and inter-connected fictional novels. Written in a uniquely constrained and minimalist style, they embrace the postmodern. Within them, he layers episodic and surreal elements into stories populated by Indigenous characters confronting the racism and bigotry common to life in Canada. Of mixed Indigenous heritage, Mr. Pruden is best described as a chronicler of the obscure captivated by a never-ending search for independence. 'Refugees of Confederation' is his sixth novel.

Manufactured by Amazon.ca
Bolton, ON